"We need to understand the details about each other if this is going to work. Otherwise, no one is going to believe we're legitimate."

"Why not?" Sam countered, and placed a soft kiss on the inside of her palm.

Julia tugged on her hand but he didn't let go. "You don't need to do that now," she whispered, her voice no more than a breath in the quiet. "There's no one watching."

One side of his mouth quirked. "It's a good thing, too, because what I want to do to you is best kept in private."

Her mouth formed a round "oh" and he lifted a finger to trace the soft flesh of her lips.

"We shouldn't…"

"I know," he repeated. "But I can't think of anything I want more."

"Me, too." She sat up and brought both of her hands to the side of his face, cupping his jaw. "This isn't going to get complicat… v, the time spent toget… e. It ends when we bo…

He agreed i… n wanted was her. He … quite yet, even if her s… going to keep the evening G-rated. So he answered, "That's the plan."

She nod… a groan. "… t her mou…

HER ACCIDENTAL ENGAGEMENT

BY
MICHELLE MAJOR

Published in Great Britain 2014
by Mills & Boon, an imprint of Harlequin (UK) Limited,
Eton House, 18-24 Paradise Road, Richmond, Surrey, TW9 1SR

ISBN: 978 0 263 91270 8

23-0314

Harlequin (UK) Limited's policy is to use papers that are natural, renewable and recyclable products and made from wood grown in sustainable forests. The logging and manufacturing processes conform to the legal environmental regulations of the country of origin.

Printed and bound in Spain
by Blackprint CPI, Barcelona

Michelle Major grew up in Ohio, but dreamed of living in the mountains. Soon after graduating with a degree in journalism, she pointed her car west and settled in Colorado. Her life and house are filled with one great husband, two beautiful kids, a few furry pets and several well-behaved reptiles. She's grateful to have found her passion writing stories with happy endings. Michelle loves to hear from her readers at www.michellemajor.com.

To Mom and Dad: for your love,
support and the years of off-key harmonies

Chapter One

Julia Morgan lit the final match, determined to destroy the letter clenched in her fingers. She was well aware of the mistakes she'd made in her life, but seeing them typed on fancy letterhead was more than she could take at the moment. She drew the flickering flame toward the paper but another gust of damp wind blew it out.

The mountains surrounding her hometown of Brevia, North Carolina, were notoriously wet in late winter. Even though it hadn't rained for several days, moisture clung to the frigid March air this afternoon, producing a cold she felt right to her bones.

With a frustrated groan, she crumpled the letter into a tiny ball. Add the inability to burn a single piece of paper to her colossal list of failures. Sinking to her knees on the soggy ground, she dropped the used matchstick into a trash bag with all the others.

She ignored the wail of a siren from the highway above

her. She'd pulled off the road minutes earlier and climbed down the steep embankment, needing a moment to stop the panic welling inside her.

For a few seconds she focused her attention on the canopy of pine trees below the ridge where she stood, her heartbeat settling to a normal rhythm.

Since she'd returned to her hometown almost two years ago, this love of the forest had surprised her. She'd never been a nature girl, her gypsy existence taking her from one big city to another. Thanks to her beautiful son, Julia was now rooted in Brevia, and the dense woods that enveloped the town gave her the sense of peace she hadn't known she'd missed for years.

The makeshift fire hadn't been much of a plan, but flying by the seat of her pants was nothing new for Julia. With a deep breath, she smoothed the wrinkled letter against the grass. She'd read it compulsively over the past week until the urge to destroy it had overtaken her. She knew the words by heart but needed the satisfaction of watching them go up in flames.

Unfit mother. Seeking custody. Better options.

Tears pricked the backs of her eyes. Burning the letter wouldn't change the potential it had to ruin her life. She'd tried to dismiss the contents as lies and conjecture. In a corner of her heart, she worried they were true and she wouldn't be able to defend herself against them.

Suddenly she was hauled to her feet. "Are you hurt? What happened?" A pair of large hands ran along her bare arms, then down her waist toward…

Whoa, there. "Back off, Andy Griffith," Julia sputtered as parts of her body she thought were in permanent hibernation sprang to life.

As if realizing how tightly he held her, Sam Callahan, Brevia's police chief, pushed away. He stalked several yards up the hill toward the road, then turned and came at her again. Muscles bunched under the shoulders of his police uniform.

She had to work hard to ignore the quick pull of awareness that pulsed through her. Darn good thing Julia had sworn off men. Even better that big, strong alpha men were *so* not her type.

Julia gave herself a mental headshake. "What do you want, Sam? I'm sort of busy here."

She could have sworn his eye twitched under his aviator sunglasses. He jabbed one arm toward the top of the hill. "What I *want* is to know what the hell you're doing off the side of the road. *Again.*"

Right. She'd forgotten that the last time Sam had found her, she'd been eight months pregnant and had wrapped her ancient Honda around a tree trunk. He'd taken her to the hospital where her son, Charlie, had been born.

That day a year and a half ago had been the start of a new life for her. One she'd protect at any cost.

Sam had been new to Brevia and the role of police chief then. He'd also been a whole lot nicer. At least, to Julia. He'd made the rounds of the single ladies in town, but ever since Charlie's birth Sam had avoided her as though he thought he might be the first man in history to catch a pregnancy. Which was fine, especially given some of the details she'd heard about his history with women.

"Julia."

At the sound of her name, she focused on his words.

"There are skid marks where your car pulled off."

"I was in a hurry," she said and swiped at her still-moist cheeks.

His hands bunched at his sides as he eyed her bag. "Do I smell smoke?"

"I lit a match. Lots of them." Her chin hitched. "Wanna call Smokey Bear for backup?"

He muttered something under his breath at the same time a semi roared by on the road above.

"I didn't quite catch that."

Sam removed his sunglasses and tucked them into the front pocket of his shirt. He was almost *too* good-looking, his blond hair short but a little messy, as if he needed a trim. The effect softened his classically handsome features and a square jaw that fell just short of comic-book chiseled. His gaze slammed into hers, and Julia knew if ice could turn molten, it would be the exact color of Sam's blue eyes.

"You were on your knees," he said slowly.

Julia swallowed. "I lost a contact."

"You don't wear contacts."

"How do you…? Never mind." She bent to retrieve the bag of worthless matches.

His finger brushed the back of her arm. "What are you doing out here, Jules?"

Something about the sound of her name soft as a whisper broke through her defenses. She straightened and waved the letter at him. "I have a meeting in town and needed some fresh air to collect my thoughts."

"At the salon?"

She shook her head. "No. Hair dye doesn't require much mental fortitude. I have a real meeting, with an attorney."

He didn't ask for details but continued to watch her.

"It's about Charlie," she offered after a minute. "About my custody." To add to her humiliation, she choked on the last word.

"You're his mother. Of course you have custody."

"I know." She lifted the letter. "But Jeff and his parents think—"

"Who's Jeff?"

"My ex-boyfriend." She sighed. "Charlie's father."

Sam's eyes narrowed. "The one who's never set eyes on him?"

"He's a college professor and travels the world doing research. His dad runs an investment firm in Columbus, Ohio, and his mom is a retired cardiologist. They're rich, powerful and very intellectual. The whole family is off-the-charts smart. I guess they have…concerns. For Charlie's future and my ability to provide the right environment. Jeff wants a new custody arrangement."

"Have Jeff's parents met Charlie?"

"No. They called a couple of times after he was born. They didn't approve of me when I was with Jeff, and since he didn't want anything to do with the baby…" She paused then added, "I let my mom deal with them."

That made him smile. "In my opinion, Vera is also off-the-charts smart."

Julia ignored the shiver in her legs at his slow grin. Her mother, Vera Morgan, was a pit bull. But also keenly intelligent. Everyone in her family was smart. Everyone but her.

"Jeff's mother is here with their family attorney to meet me. To make sure everything's okay—that Charlie is in good hands."

"Of course he's in good hands." Sam's voice gentled as he repeated, "You're his mother."

"I've done a lot of stupid things in my life, made a lot of mistakes. Jeff knows the sordid details and I'm sure his parents do, too." Emotion clogged her throat.

Sam was not the man she wanted to have see her like this. She made a show of checking her watch. "What I could use is some damage control for my reputation. White picket fence, doting husband, pillar of the community stuff. It's a little late for me to join the Junior League." She shook her head. "Anyway, thanks for your concern today, but as you can see, I'm peachy keen."

"You shouldn't talk to anyone until you get an attorney of your own."

"Frank Davis said he would help me, but I hope it won't come to that. I'm sure the Johnsons want what's best for Charlie. I should at least hear them out. That boy deserves everything this world has to offer." She gave a humorless laugh and started back toward the road. "What he's got is me."

As she moved past Sam, his hand reached out, but she jerked away. If he touched her right now she'd be a goner, and she needed to keep it together. For Charlie.

"You're more than enough," he called after her.

"From your lips to God's ears, Chief," she whispered and climbed up to her car.

"Who are you and what have you done with my father?"

Sam shifted in his chair at Carl's, Brevia's most popular restaurant, still reeling from his unbelievable afternoon. From the bizarre encounter with Julia he'd been called to a domestic disturbance that ended up being a chicken loose in Bobby Royall's kitchen. It had made him almost thirty minutes late to dinner with his dad. Now he wished the bird hadn't been so easy to catch.

Joe Callahan adjusted his Patriots baseball cap and chuckled. "It's me, son. Only better."

Said who?

His father had been a police officer in Boston for almost forty years, most of which had been spent working homicide. Joe Callahan had dedicated his life to his career, and his family had suffered from the on-the-job stress and risks he took daily. Although it wasn't intentional, Sam had modeled his own life after his father's. Sam had put his job before everything and everyone in his life—just like Joe.

Recently, though, Joe had begun conducting programs for police departments on emotional awareness. Sam had resisted his father's repeated attempts to help him "get in touch" with his feelings. But now Joe was here and impossible to ignore.

"The boys down at the precinct loved my seminar. At least four of 'em were in tears by the end. I got thank-you notes from a half-dozen wives."

"That's great, Dad." Sam took a long drink of iced tea, wishing he wasn't on duty. A cold one would be mighty helpful tonight. "I don't see what that has to do with me or your unexpected visit to Brevia."

His father pulled a flyer out of the briefcase at his feet and pushed it across the table. "While I'm down here, I thought we could organize a workshop."

Sam glanced at the pamphlet. His stomach gave a hearty gurgle. *Law with Love, Presented by Retired Police Captain Joseph Callahan.* A picture of Joe hugging a group of uniformed officers filled the front page. Sam couldn't remember ever being hugged by his craggy, hard-nosed father. Holy mother of…

"I don't know. It's only me and one deputy on the force."

Joe tapped the sheet of paper. "It's for firefighters and paramedics, too. We could bring in neighboring towns—make it a regional event. Plus civil servants, city council. You're looking at a long-term reappointment, right? This could make quite an impression as far as your potential."

At the mention of his possible future in Brevia, Sam lost the battle with his temper. "My potential as what? I'm the chief of police, not the hug-it-out type."

His father's sharp intake of breath made Sam regret

his outburst. "Sorry. You know what a small town this is and—"

Joe held up a hand. "Don't apologize." He removed his bifocals and dabbed at his eyes with a napkin.

"You aren't going to cry," Sam muttered, disbelieving. "You don't cry."

"Yes. I *am* going to cry. To take a moment and *feel* my pain."

Great. This was the second time today he'd brought someone to tears.

After a loud nose blow, Joe's watery gaze met his. "I feel my pain, and I feel yours."

"I'm not in pain." Sam let his eyes drift shut. "Other than a raging headache."

Joe ignored him and continued, "I did this to you, Sammy."

Sammy? His father hadn't called him Sammy since—

"When your mother died my whole world collapsed. I didn't think I could live without her. I didn't want to. It broke me a little more every day to see you and your brother that sad. I did the only thing I could to survive. I shut off my heart, and I made you do the same. I was wrong. I'm here to make it right again."

Sam saw customers from the surrounding tables begin to stare. "It's okay. Let's go outside for a minute."

Joe followed Sam's gaze and shook his head. "I'm not embarrassed to show my feelings. Not anymore." He took another breath, this one steadier. "Ever since the incident with my ole ticker." He thumped his sweatshirt. "They say facing death can make you reevaluate your whole life."

"It was indigestion, Dad. Not a real heart attack. Remember?"

"Doesn't matter. The change to my heart was real. The

effect on my life was real." He readjusted his glasses. "I want the same change for you. I want you to be happy."

"I'm fine." Sam gulped a mouthful of ice and crunched. "Happy as a clam."

"Are you seeing anyone?"

Alarm bells went off in Sam's head. "I…sure…am actually. She's great." He looked away from his father's expectant face, unable to lie to him directly. He glanced around the crowded restaurant and his gaze landed on Julia at a booth in the back. He hadn't noticed her when he'd first walked in, but now he couldn't pull his eyes away.

This must be the meeting with her ex-boyfriend's family she'd told him about. The faces of the two women seated across from her were blocked, but Julia's cheeks flamed pink. Her palm smacked the table as if she was about to lose control.

Easy there, sweetheart, he counseled silently.

As if she'd heard him, her eyes met his and held for several moments. His pulse hammered against his throat. Then she squared her shoulders and folded her hands in her lap.

He turned back to his father. "You'd like her. She's a real spitfire."

Joe smiled. "Like your mother."

Sam forced himself not to look at Julia again. "I was ten when she died. I don't remember that much."

"This one's different than your other girls?"

Sam caught the waitress's attention and signaled for the check.

"Because I think you need a new perspective. After what happened with…"

"I don't want to rehash my relationship history."

Joe reached across the table and clasped Sam's hand in his. "I know you want to find love and settle down."

Sam heard a loud cough behind him and found the young waitress staring. Her look could only be described as predatory. *Fantastic.* Sam had dated some when he'd first come to town but had kept to himself recently, finding it easier and less complicated to be alone. The way gossip went viral in Brevia, he'd have a fresh line of eligible women in front of his office by morning.

"I told you," Sam said, loud enough for the waitress to hear. "I've got a girlfriend. We're very happy."

The waitress dropped the check on the table with a *humph* and stalked away.

"It's serious?" Joe asked.

Sam's gaze wandered to Julia again. "Very," he muttered as she jabbed a finger across the table. This time his mental warning to not lose control didn't reach her. Her voice grew so loud that people at surrounding tables turned.

"I want to meet her," his dad said, rubbing his palms together, oblivious to the commotion behind him. "Why don't you give her a call and see if she can meet us for dessert? If she's so wonderful, I can help make sure you don't blow it."

At the moment, Sam wasn't worried about screwing up anything himself or producing a nonexistent girlfriend for his dad to fawn over. Instead he felt the need to avert someone else's disaster. "I'll be right back."

Joe grabbed his arm as he started past. "Don't be sore, Sammy. I was joking. You're a great catch."

Sam shrugged out of his father's grasp. "I need a minute. Stay here."

He darted around a passing waiter as he made his way to Julia, who now stood in front of the booth.

"You have no idea what I'm capable of," she shouted. All eyes on this side of the restaurant were glued to her.

Just as he reached her, Julia picked up a glass of water from the table. Sam leaned in and wrapped his fingers around hers before she could hurl it at anyone.

"Hey there, sugar," he said as he pulled her tense body tight to his side. "I didn't realize your meeting was at Carl's tonight. You doing okay?"

"Let go of me," she said on a hiss of breath. "This is none of your concern."

"Well, I *am* concerned," he whispered then plastered on a wide smile. "I haven't met your new friends yet."

She squirmed against him. "They aren't my—"

"Howdy, folks," Sam interrupted, turning his attention to the two strangers staring at him. "I'm Sam Callahan. A...uh...friend of Julia's."

The woman in the corner practically screamed "old money," from her sophisticated haircut to her tailored suit. A thick strand of pearls hung around her neck and a massive diamond sparkled on her left hand. The way her gaze narrowed, she must be Charlie's paternal grandmother. Next to her was a younger woman, tiny and bookish. Her big owl eyes blinked from behind retro glasses. Faint streaks of color stole up her neck from the collar of her starched oxford shirt as she watched the two of them.

"Friend?" The older woman scoffed. "Latest conquest, no doubt." She nudged the woman beside her. "Are you taking notes on this? She's now flaunting her boy toy in front of us."

Boy toy? Sam's smile vanished and he worked to keep his voice pleasant. "Excuse me, ma'am, you have the wrong idea—"

She continued as if he hadn't spoken. "Can you imagine what my grandson's been subjected to when his mother is obviously a tramp? When the judge hears—"

Sam held up a hand. "Wait just one minute, lady. If you think you can waltz in here—"

Julia's fingernails dug into his arm. "I *don't* need your help. Walk away."

He glanced down at her and saw embarrassment shimmering along with anger in her expression. And fear. At the mention of the word *judge,* he'd felt some of the fight go out of her. He wished he hadn't interrupted, that he'd let her handle her own problems, the way she'd wanted to in the first place. But a part of Sam needed to be the hero just so he could feel something. It was what he was used to, one of the few things he could count on. That part of him couldn't walk away.

He released Julia and leveled his best law-enforcement stare at the grandmother. As he expected, she shrank back and darted a nervous glance at her companion. "I'm Sam Callahan, Brevia's police chief." Hands on hips, he held her gaze. "To be clear, I am *no one's* boy toy and would appreciate if you'd conduct yourself in a more civilized manner in my town. We don't take kindly to strangers spreading malicious rumors about our own. Do I make myself clear?"

Several beats passed before the studious-looking woman cleared her throat. "Mr. Callahan—"

Sam squared his shoulders. "You can call me Chief."

The attorney swallowed. "Chief Callahan, I'm Lexi Preston. I represent the interests of Charlie Morgan's father, Jeff Johnson, and grandparents, Dennis and Maria Johnson. My father is the Johnsons' family attorney and he asked me—"

"Get to the point."

"Yes, well…" Lexi mumbled as she shuffled papers around the table. "I was simply explaining to Ms. Morgan the facts of her case, or lack thereof, when she became hostile and confrontational. My client is not to blame for this unfortunate disturbance. We have statements from a number of Ms. Morgan's former acquaintances as to her character, so Dr. Johnson's assertion, while ill-advised, is not without foundation."

He heard Julia suck in a breath but kept his attention on the two women. "I don't care what your so-called statements allege. You're not going to drag Julia's name through the mud."

Preston collected the rest of the papers. "Why is Ms. Morgan's reputation your business? Is she under investigation by local law enforcement?"

"This can't get any worse," Julia whispered so low only he could here. "Go away, Sam. Now."

From the corner of his eye, Sam saw his father standing a few feet away, watching him intently. Sam was a good cop and he played things by the book, having learned the hard way not to bite off more than he could chew.

But some lessons didn't stick.

He peeled Julia's hand from its death grip around his upper arm and laced her fingers with his. "It's my business, Counselor, because I'm not going to let you or anyone hurt the woman I intend to marry."

Chapter Two

Julia thought things couldn't get worse.

Until they did.

She glanced around the restaurant, as dumbfounded as the people who stared at her from the surrounding tables. She recognized a lot of them; Carl's was a popular spot for Brevia locals.

Yanking Sam away from the table a few steps, she smiled up into his face, well aware of their audience. It took all her willpower to resist the urge to slap him silly. "Have you lost your mind?" she said, keeping her voice low.

The corners of his mouth were tight as he returned her smile. "Apparently."

"Fix this. You have to fix this."

"That's what I'm trying to do." He smoothed a stray hair from her cheek. "Trust me."

No way. Julia didn't trust men. She had a long line of

heartbreak in her past. Mountains of collateral damage that made her sure she was the only person she could trust to take care of her and Charlie. "Don't touch me," she whispered through gritted teeth.

His hand dropped from her face. "I'm going to help you. But you can't fight me. Not here."

She glanced over his shoulder at the attorney and Charlie's grandmother. For a fraction of a second, worry marred Maria Johnson's perfect features. Julia didn't understand the break in the ice queen's armor, but it must have had something to do with Sam.

"Fine." She reached forward and clasped both of his rock-solid arms, as if she could make him understand the gravity of her situation through a simple squeeze. "You better make it count. Charlie's future is on the line."

He searched her gaze for a long moment, then bent onto one knee. He took her fingers in his, tugging softly when she would have pulled away.

"I didn't mean…"

"Julia Morgan," he said, and his deep, clear voice rang out in the restaurant. "We've kept this quiet—no easy task in Brevia—but it's long past time to make things official." He cleared his throat, adjusting the collar of his starched uniform shirt. "Would you do me the honor of becoming my wife?"

Julia blinked back sudden tears. A marriage proposal was what she'd wanted, once upon a time. She'd wanted Jeff to see they could build a real life together. Foolishly sure he was the one, she'd been reckless and selfish. Then the universe had blessed her with a beautiful son. She was working day and night to make a good life for Charlie. Now that she wanted to do the right thing, she risked losing him.

Not for the first time, she wondered if he'd be better off

with the Johnsons and the privileged life filled with opportunities they could provide.

She squeezed her eyes shut to clear her thoughts. She was Charlie's mother, no matter what, and wouldn't ever stop fighting for him.

Sam ran his finger along the inside of her wrist. "Are you going to answer the question? My leg is cramping."

"Oh, no. Sorry."

"No?" he asked over the collective gasp.

"I mean yes. Get up, you big oaf." Heat flooded her face and her stomach churned. What was she doing? She'd learned not to rely on a man for anything and now she was putting her entire future in Sam's hands. Impulsive as ever, she repeated, "Yes. My answer is yes."

He stood, rubbing one knee. "Cool it on the name-calling. We're in love, remember."

"You betcha, honey-bunny."

That produced a genuine grin from him, and she was again caught off guard by her body's reaction as tiny butterflies did a fast samba across her belly. Oblivious to his effect on her, Sam turned to the booth.

Before he could speak, an older man wrapped them both in a tight hug. "This is amazing."

Amazing? Not quite.

Sam caught her gaze, his eyes dark and unreadable. "I forgot to tell you earlier. My dad came to town today. Meet Joe Callahan, your future father-in-law."

Uh-oh.

Joe cupped her face between his large hands. "You're just what he needed. I can already tell." Tears shimmered in eyes the same color as Sam's, only sweeter and looking at her with such kindness a lump formed in Julia's throat. "You remind me of my Lorraine, rest her soul."

"Okay, Dad." Sam tugged her out of Joe's embrace. She took a step back but Sam pulled her against his side.

Joe turned to the booth. "I'll buy a round to celebrate. Any friends of..."

"Julia," Sam supplied with a sigh.

"Any friends of my future daughter-in-law are friends of mine."

"We're *not* friends," Lexi Preston ground out. "As I said earlier, I represent her son's biological father and his parents. They're interested in exploring a more viable custody arrangement. The Johnsons want what's best for the child. They can give him opportunities—"

"They want to take my baby," Julia mumbled. Sam's arm tightened around her waist.

If Joe was surprised to hear she had a child, he didn't let on. His posture went rigid. "That's ridiculous. She's the boy's mother."

"Dad, this isn't the time or place—" Sam began.

Joe wagged a finger at Lexi Preston and Maria Johnson. "Now listen here. I don't know what all this nonsense is about, but I can tell you my son will take care of that child and Julia. He's the law around here, for heaven's sake." He leaned closer and Lexi's nervous swallow mimicked Julia's. Joe Callahan might look like a teddy bear but he had a backbone of steel. "You'll have to come through both of us if you try to hurt her. We protect our own."

"I've had quite enough of this town for tonight." Maria pushed at the attorney, who stood quickly. "I don't care who you've got in your backwater little corner of the world, we're going to—"

Lexi put a hand on Maria's shoulder to silence her. "The less said tonight, the better. We have a court date next week." She gave Julia a curt nod. "Ms. Morgan, we'll see you then."

"Take care of the check, Lexi." Maria Johnson barked the order at her attorney before stalking out of the restaurant.

"Does that mean she's leaving Brevia?" Julia asked.

"For now. I'll stay for the duration of the process. The Johnsons will fly back and forth." Lexi leaned toward Julia. "I don't want to get your hopes up, but a stable home environment could change the situation." She clapped a hand over her mouth as if she'd said too much, then nodded to the group and scurried away.

Julia reached forward to hug Joe. "Thank you, Mr. Callahan. For what you said."

"I meant it. Sam isn't going to let anything happen to you."

Sam.

Julia turned, but focused her attention on the badge pinned to Sam's beige shirt, unable to make eye contact with him. Instead she looked out at the tables surrounding them. "Sorry for the commotion. Go back to dinner, and we'll get out of your way."

"Wait a minute." Sam's voice cut through the quiet.

Julia held her breath.

"As most of you heard tonight, Julia and I have something to celebrate." He grabbed her hand and drew her back to him. Her fingers spread across his broad chest of their own accord. "We need to make this believable for the gossip mill," he whispered against her ear.

A round of applause rang out in the restaurant followed by several clinks on glasses. "Kiss. Kiss. Kiss," came the call from the bar.

Julia froze as Sam gazed down at her, his expression heated. "Better give them what they want."

"It's totally unbelievable and I had garlic for dinner," she muttered, squirming in his arms.

"I'll take my chances," he answered with a laugh.

"Have it your way." Cheeks burning, she raised her head and pressed her mouth to his, a chaste peck fit for the balcony at Buckingham Palace. When she would have ended the kiss, Sam caught hold of her neck and dipped her low. She let out a startled gasp and he slid his tongue against the seam of her lips. Ever so gently he molded his mouth to hers.

A fire sparked low in her belly as she breathed in the scent of him, warm and woodsy and completely male. Lost in her reaction, her arms wound around his neck and her fingers played in the short hair along his collar. She heard his sharp intake of breath and suddenly he righted them both to a chorus of catcalls and stomping feet.

"That's what I'm talking about," someone yelled.

"Okay, folks." Sam's gaze swept across the restaurant and he smiled broadly. "Show's over. I'm going to see my lovely bride-to-be home."

Julia pressed her fingers to her lips and looked at Sam. The smile didn't reach his eyes.

When she turned, Joe watched her. "You're a breath of fresh air if I ever saw one," he said and gave her trembling hand a squeeze.

She led the group into the night but not before she noticed several members of the ladies' auxiliary huddled in the corner. They'd have a field day with this one. The salon would be buzzing with the news by morning. Her chest tightened as she felt Sam behind her, frustration pouring off him like a late-winter rainstorm. Maybe he'd already come to regret his stupid proposal.

This entire situation was his fault. She'd told him she didn't need a hero, and that was the truth.

Still, his announcement had rattled Maria Johnson and

her attorney. She couldn't figure out how a fake engagement would benefit Sam, but he wasn't her problem.

Charlie was Julia's only priority. She'd do anything for her son.

Right now she needed time to think, to figure out how to make this bizarre predicament work in her favor. "It's been a long day, boys," she said quickly. "Joe, it was nice to meet you. How long will you be—"

"We need to talk," Sam interrupted, gripping her arm when she tried to break away.

"I thought I'd be around for a while. Give my boy some lessons in tapping into his feelings, finding his passion and all that." Joe gave Sam a hearty thump on the back. "After that little display, I think he may have wised up on his own. You're good for him, Julia. Real good."

Sam's hold on her loosened. He studied his father. "You mean one kiss convinced you I can do without a dose of your emotional mumbo jumbo?"

Julia swatted his arm. "That's your father. Show some respect."

Sam shot her a withering look. "I'll remember that the next time your mom's around."

Joe laughed and wrapped them in another hug. "Not just any kiss. It's different when you kiss *the one.* Trust me, I know. I bet they could see the sparks flying between the two of you clear down to the coast."

Looking into Joe's trusting face, she couldn't let Sam's father pin his hopes on her. She had to tell him the truth.

"Mr. Callahan, I don't—"

"You're right, Dad," Sam agreed. "It's different with Julia. I'm different, and I don't want you to worry about me anymore." He pinched the tip of Julia's nose, a little harder than necessary if you asked her.

"Ouch."

"Such a delicate flower." He laughed and dropped a quick kiss on her forehead. "What would I do without you?"

"Troll for women over in Charlotte?" she offered.

"See why I need her by my side?"

Joe nodded. "I do."

Sam turned to Julia and rubbed his warm hands down her arms. "Where are you parked?"

Julia pointed to the blue Jetta a few spaces down from where they stood, her mind still reeling.

"Perfect. I'm going to walk Dad back to the hotel and we'll talk tomorrow."

She didn't like the look in his eye. "I'm kind of busy at the salon tomorrow."

"Never too busy for your one true love."

Julia stifled the urge to gag. "I guess not."

"Get going, then, sugar." He pinched her bottom, making her yelp. She rounded on him but, at the calculating gleam in his eye, turned back toward her car. Sam and his dad watched until she'd pulled out.

Despite this peculiar evening, his announcement had served its purpose. Lexi Preston had said having Sam in the picture might change things. That could be the understatement of the year, but if it kept Charlie safe, Julia would make it work.

No matter what.

Sam took a fortifying drink of coffee and watched as another woman walked through the door of The Best Little Hairhouse. He knew Julia had worked at the salon since her return to Brevia two years ago, but that wasn't why he avoided this place like the plague. It was too girlie for him. The bottles of hair product and little rows of nail polish on the shelves gave him the heebie-jeebies.

The one time he'd ventured into the Hairhouse, after the owner had reported a man lurking in the back alley, he'd felt like a prize steer come up for auction.

He adjusted the brim of his hat, buttoned his jacket against the late-morning rain and started across the street. He'd put the visit off until almost lunchtime, irritated with himself at how much he wanted to see Julia again. Part of him wanted to blame her for making him crazy, but another piece, the part he tried to ignore, wanted to get close enough to her to smell the scent of sunshine on her hair.

He scrubbed a hand across his face. Sunshine on her hair? What the hell was that about? Women didn't smell like sunshine. She worked at a salon and probably had a ton of gunk in her hair at any given moment. Although the way the strands had felt soft on his fingers when he'd bent to kiss her last night told another story.

One he wasn't interested in reading. Or so he told himself.

Sam opened the front door and heard a blood-curdling scream from behind the wall at the reception desk. He jerked to attention. He might not spend a lot of time in beauty salons but could guarantee that sound wasn't typical.

"I'm going to choke the life out of her," a woman yelled, "as soon as my nails dry."

Nope. Something wasn't right.

He glanced at the empty reception desk then stepped through the oversized doorway that led to the main room.

A pack of women huddled around one of the chairs, Julia in the center of the mix.

"Is there a problem here, ladies?"

Seven pairs of eyes, ranging from angry to horrified, turned to him.

"Sam, thank the Lord you're here."

"You would not believe what happened."

"Congrats on your engagement, Chief."

The last comment produced silence from the group. He met Julia's exasperated gaze. "Not a good time," she mouthed and turned back to the center of the cluster, only to be pushed aside by a woman with a black smock draped around her considerable girth. Sam tried not to gape at her head, where the neat curls framing her face glowed an iridescent pink.

"There will be time for celebrating later. I want that woman arrested," Ida Garvey announced. Sam was used to Ida issuing dictatorial commands. She was the wealthiest woman in town, thanks to a generous inheritance from her late husband. Other than the clown hair, she looked like a picture-perfect grandma, albeit one with a sharp tongue and a belief that she ruled the world.

For an instant, he thought she was pointing at Julia. Then he noticed the young woman hunched in the corner, furiously wiping tears from her cheeks.

"Ida, don't be a drama queen." Julia shook her head. "No one is being arrested. Accidents happen. We'll fix it, but—"

"She turned my hair pink!" With a screech, Ida vaulted from the chair and grabbed a curling iron from a stand. "I'm going to kill her!" Ida lunged toward the cowering woman, but Julia stepped into her path. The curling iron dropped, the barrel landing on Julia's arm before clattering to the floor.

Julia bit out an oath and Ida screamed again. "Look what you made me do," she bellowed at the now-sobbing stylist. "I burned her."

Sam strode forward with a new appreciation for the simplicity of breaking up a drunken bar brawl. Ida looked into his face then staggered back, one hand fluttering to her chest. "Are you gonna arrest me, Chief?"

"Sit down, Mrs. Garvey." He waved at the group of women. "All of you, back off. Now."

Ida plopped back into the chair as the group fell silent again.

Julia winced as he took her arm in his hands. A crimson mark slashed across her wrist, the skin already raised and angry. "Where's a faucet?"

"I'm fine," she said through gritted teeth. "Happens all the time."

"I sure as hell hope not."

"Not exactly like this. I can use the sink in back." She tugged her arm but he didn't let go.

"Don't anyone move," he ordered the women. "That means you, Ida."

"I don't need your help," Julia ground out as he followed her to the back of the salon.

"You aren't leaving me alone with that crowd."

"Not so brave now." Julia fumbled with the tap.

He nudged her out of the way. "I'll do it. Nice ring. I have good taste."

"I had it from… Well, it doesn't matter." Her cheeks flamed as she glanced at the diamond sparkling on her left hand. "I thought I should wear something until we had a chance to figure things out. Fewer questions that way. You know how nosy people are, especially in the salon."

They needed to talk, but Sam couldn't get beyond Julia being hurt, even by a curling iron. "Tell me what happened."

"Crystal, the one in the corner, is our newest stylist. Ida came in without an appointment and she was the only one available. When she went to mix the color, Ida started barking orders. Crystal got so nervous, she mixed it wrong.

Instead of a fluffy white cotton ball, Mrs. Garvey's head is now glowing neon pink."

Sam hid a smile as he drew her arm under the faucet and adjusted the temperature. She closed her eyes and sighed as cold water washed over the burn. He drew small circles on her palm, amazed at the softness of her skin under the pad of his thumb.

After a moment he asked, "Do you want to press charges?"

Her eyes flew open, and then she smiled at his expression. "Assault with a deadly styling tool? No, thanks."

Her smile softened the angles of her face, made her beauty less ethereal and more earthy. God help him, he loved earthy.

She must have read something in his eyes because she yanked her hand away and flipped off the water. "I need to get out there before Ida goes after Crystal again."

"Did you hire Crystal?"

"About three weeks ago. She came over from Memphis right out of school to stay with her aunt and needs a break…" She paused, her eyes narrowing. "You think I'm an idiot for hiring a girl with so little experience."

"I didn't say that."

"Everyone thinks Val's a fool to leave me in charge. They're waiting for me to mess up." She wrapped her arms around her waist then flinched when the burn touched her sweater. "And here I am."

Sam knew Val Dupree, the Hairhouse's longtime owner, was planning to retire, and Julia was working to secure a loan to buy the business. She was acting as the salon's manager while Val spent the winter in Florida. "No one expects you to mess up."

"You've been in town long enough to know what people think of me."

The words held no malice, but she said them with a

quiet conviction. Sam wanted to take her in his arms to soothe her worry and at the same time shake some sense into her. "Was it a mistake to hire Crystal?"

"No." She looked at him as though she expected an argument. When he offered none she continued, "She's good. Or she will be. I know it."

"Then we'd better make sure Ida Garvey doesn't attack your future star again."

"Right." She led him back into the main salon, where Ida still pinned Crystal to the wall with her angry stare. Everyone else's attention was fixed on Julia and Sam.

Julia glanced over her shoulder. "It's been twenty questions about our relationship all morning."

He nodded. "Let's take on one disaster at a time."

She squared her shoulders and approached Mrs. Garvey, no trace of self-doubt evident. "Ida, I'm sorry." She bent in front of the chair and took the older woman's hands in hers. "I'm going to clear my schedule for the afternoon and make your hair better than before. You'll get three months' worth of free services for your trouble."

Mrs. Garvey patted her pink hair. "That would help."

"Lizzy?" Julia called. A young woman peeked around the doorway from the front of the salon. "Would you reschedule the rest of my clients? Everyone else, back to work."

"I'm sorry," Crystal said from the corner, taking a step toward Julia.

Ida shifted in the chair. "Don't you come near me."

Sam moved forward but Julia simply patted Ida's fleshy arm. "Take the rest of the day off, Crystal. I'll see you back here in the morning."

"Day off?" Ida screeched. "You're going to fire her, aren't you? Val would have fired her on the spot!"

Color rose in Julia's cheeks but she held her ground. "No, Mrs. Garvey. Crystal made a mistake."

"She's a menace. I knew she was doing it wrong from the start."

"She made a mistake," Julia repeated. "In part because you didn't let her do her job." She looked at Crystal. "Go on, hon. We'll talk in the morning."

"I have half a mind to call Val Dupree this minute and tell her how you're going to run her business into the ground."

"I'd watch what you say right now, Mrs. Garvey." Sam pointed to her hair. "Julia may leave you pink if you're not careful."

"She wouldn't dare." But Ida shut her mouth, chewing furiously on her bottom lip.

"Get comfortable," Julia told her. "We'll be here for a while."

She turned to Sam. "I think your work here is done, Chief."

He leveled a steely look at her. "We're not finished."

"Unless you want to pull up a chair next to Ida we are. The longer that color sits on her hair, the harder time I'll have getting it out."

"You don't play fair."

Her eyes glinted. "I never have."

Chapter Three

Julia rubbed her nose against Charlie's dimpled neck and was rewarded by a soft belly laugh. "Who's my best boy?" she asked and kissed the top of his head.

"Charlie," he answered in his sweet toddler voice.

"Thanks for keeping him today, Lainey." Julia's younger sister and their mother, Vera, took turns watching Charlie on the days when his normal babysitter was unavailable. "Things were crazy today at work."

She couldn't imagine balancing everything without her family's help. Two years ago, Julia's relationship with Lainey had been almost nonexistent. Thanks in large part to Charlie, she now felt a sisterly bond she hadn't realized was missing from her life.

"Crazy, how?" Lainey asked from where she stirred a pot of soup at the stove.

"Ida Garvey ended up with hair so pink it looked like cotton candy."

Lainey's mouth dropped open.

"She freaked out, as you can imagine." Charlie scrambled off her lap to play with a toy fire truck on the kitchen floor. "It took the whole afternoon to make it better."

"I thought you meant crazy like telling people about your secret boyfriend and his public proposal." Lainey turned and pointed a wooden spoon at Julia as if it were a weapon. "I can't believe I didn't even know you two were dating."

Julia groaned at the accusation in her sister's tone and the hurt that shadowed her green eyes. When she'd gone along with Sam's fake proposal last night, Julia hadn't thought about the repercussions of people believing them. Thinking things through wasn't her strong suit.

She didn't talk about her years away from Brevia with Lainey or their mother. They had some inkling of her penchant for dating losers and changing cities at the end of each bad relationship. When the going got tough, it had always seemed easier to move on than stick it out.

From the outside, Julia knew she appeared to have it together. She was quick with a sarcastic retort that made people believe life's little setbacks didn't affect her. She'd painted herself as the free spirit who wouldn't be tied to anyone or any place.

But her devil-may-care mask hid a deeply rooted insecurity that, if someone really got to know her, she wouldn't measure up. Because of her learning disabilities and in so many other ways.

Her struggles to read and process numbers at the most basic level had defined who she was for years. The shame she felt, as a result, was part of the very fiber of her being. She'd been labeled stupid and lazy, and despite what anyone told her to the contrary, she couldn't shake the belief that it was true.

Maybe that was why she picked men who were obviously bad bets. Maybe that was why she'd been a mean girl in high school—to keep people at arm's length so she wouldn't have a chance of being rejected.

She wondered for a moment how it would feel to confide the entire complicated situation to Lainey. For one person to truly understand her problem. She ached to lean in for support as fear weighed on her heart. But as much as they'd worked to repair their fractured relationship, Julia still couldn't tell her sister how scared she was of failing at what meant the most to her in life: being a mother to Charlie.

"I'm sorry. I didn't mean for half the town to find out at Carl's." No one in her family even knew about Jeff's interest in a new custody arrangement.

She stood, trying to come up with a plausible reason she wouldn't have shared big boyfriend news. "My track record with guys is common knowledge, and I didn't want Sam to have people beating down his door to warn him away from me."

Lainey's gaze turned sympathetic. "Oh, Jules. When Ethan and I first got back together I didn't want anyone to know, either. I felt like the town would hold my past mistakes against me and you were back and… Never mind now. I'm going to forgive you because it's so wonderful." She threw her arms around Julia. "Everyone loves Sam, so…" Lainey's voice trailed off.

Julia's stomach turned with frustration. "So, what? By default people are suddenly going to open their arms to me?"

Lainey shrugged. "It can't hurt. Do you have a date?"

"For what?"

Lainey pushed away. "The wedding, silly. You'll get married in Brevia, right?"

Julia blinked. "I suppose so. We're taking the planning slowly. I want a long engagement. It'll be better for Charlie."

"Sure." Lainey frowned but went back to the stove.

"Just enjoying each other and all that," Julia added quickly, guilt building with every lie she told. "So in love. You know."

"I want to be involved in the planning."

"Of course. We can have a girls' day out to look for dresses and stuff." With each detail, the difficulty of deceiving her family became more apparent.

She reminded herself that it was only for a short time, and she was protecting everyone from the stress of the custody fight. "I should go. Thanks to the commotion today, I'm late on the product order I should have sent. If Charlie goes down early enough, I'll be able to get it in tomorrow morning. A night full of numbers, lucky me."

"Do you want some help?"

Julia tensed. "I can handle it. I'm not a total idiot, despite rumors to the contrary." She saw hurt flash again in her sister's gaze and regretted her defensive tone.

She did most of the paperwork for the salon when Charlie went to bed to minimize her hours away from him. She spent many late nights pouring over the accounts and payroll information, terrified she'd make a mistake or miss an important detail. She was determined no one would ever see how unqualified she was to run her own business.

"No one thinks you're an idiot," Lainey said quietly. "You're doing an amazing job with the salon, but I know how things get when you're tired. I'm offering another set of eyes if you need them."

"I'm sorry I snapped." Julia rubbed two fingers against each temple, trying to ward off an impending headache.

"I'll take it slow. It's routine paperwork, not splitting the atom."

"Could you delegate some of this to the receptionist or one of the part-time girls? Why does it all have to fall on you? If you'd only tell them—"

"They can't know. No one can. What if Val found out? The deal isn't final. She could change her mind about selling to me."

"She wouldn't do that," Lainey argued.

"Someone could take advantage, mix things up without me understanding until it's too late." Julia gathered Charlie's sippy cup and extra snacks into the diaper bag.

Lainey shook her head, frustration evident as she fisted her hands at her sides. "Learning disabilities don't make you stupid, Julia. When are you going to realize that? Your brain processes information differently. It has nothing to do with your IQ, and you have the best intuition of anyone I know. No one could take advantage of you—"

"Have you seen my list of ex-boyfriends?"

"—without you letting them," Lainey finished.

"Point taken." Even as much as Julia had wanted her relationship with Jeff to work out, she should have known it was doomed. He'd been the opposite of most guys she'd dated, and she should have known someone so academic and cultured wouldn't truly want her. They'd gone to museums and gallery openings, his interest in her giving her hope that someone would finally see her for more than a pretty face.

She'd craved his approval and made the mistake of sharing her secret with him. None of the men before him had known about the severe learning disabilities that had plagued her since grade school. She'd managed for years to keep her LD hidden from almost everyone.

Only her family and certain trusted teachers had known

the struggles she'd faced in learning to read and process both words and numbers. She wasn't sure any of them understood how deep her problems were. The embarrassment and frustrations she'd felt as a kid had prevented her from letting teachers, interventionists or even her parents truly help her.

It had been easier to play the part of being too cool for school or, as she got older, not wanting to be tied down to a real job or responsibilities. Only for Charlie was she finally willing to put her best effort forward, constantly worried it wouldn't be enough.

"Are you still working with the literacy specialist?"

"Every week. It's a slow process, though. Between my visual and auditory learning deficiencies, I feel like a lost cause. Sometimes I wonder if it's even worth it."

"It's worth it," Lainey said as she lifted Charlie from the floor and gave him a hug before depositing him into Julia's arms. "LD is complex and I'm proud of you for everything you've accomplished despite it. I'm here if you need me. Ethan and Mom can take Charlie, so—"

"Mom's back?" Julia swallowed. She'd assumed her sister hadn't heard about the engagement. But their mother had her finger on the pulse of every snippet of gossip from Brevia to the state line. "She wasn't scheduled back until next week." Long enough for Julia to get a handle on her mess of a life.

"She flew in this morning. I can help contain her, you know. You'll need reinforcements for damage control on that front."

Julia stopped in her tracks. Even though she'd worried about her mother finding out, hearing Lainey say it made her knees quiver the tiniest bit. "Mom knows? I thought she just got back."

"She knows," Lainey answered with an eye roll. "I think she's waiting for you to call and explain yourself."

Another layer of dread curled in the pit of Julia's stomach. Her mother would support her. Vera was a big part of Charlie's life and would fight tooth and nail to protect him. But she understood Julia's limitations better than anyone. Julia didn't want to know if her mom had any doubts about her ability to give Charlie a good life on her own.

Now was the time to come clean, but with Charlie in her arms, she couldn't bring herself to voice her fears. It might make them too real.

"I'll call her. She'll understand. I'll make her understand."

Lainey only smiled. "Good luck."

Julia needed a lot more than luck.

She tried to ignore the persistent knocking at her apartment door later that night. She hadn't called her mother and silently debated whether Vera would make the twenty-minute drive to Julia's apartment to rake her over the coals in person.

But Charlie had just fallen asleep after six verses of "The Wheels on the Bus," and Julia wasn't going to risk the noise waking him, so she opened the door, prepared for the mother–daughter smackdown of the century.

Sam stood in the hallway watching her.

Even better.

"Long day, Chief. I'll call you tomorrow." She tried to close the door but he shoved his foot into the opening. Blast those steel-toed boots.

He held up a white cardboard box and a six-pack of beer. "It's been a long day for both of us. We eat first and then dig ourselves out of this mess."

She sniffed the air. "Pepperoni?"

"With extra cheese."

She took a step back and he eased around her into the tiny apartment. It actually didn't feel so small with just her and Charlie in it. Somehow, Sam not only filled the room but used more than his fair share of the oxygen in it. Julia drew a shaky breath and led the way to the small dining area.

"Sorry," she apologized automatically as she picked macaroni noodles from the maple tabletop. "Charlie's been practicing his QB skills at mealtime."

"Nothing wrong with starting early. Where's the little guy?"

"Asleep. Finally."

Sam put the box on the table and handed her a beer as he cocked his head. "Is that classical music?"

"Beethoven."

"Sounds different than I remember. More animated."

She picked up a remote and pointed it at the television on the other side of the room. "It's a Junior Genius DVD."

"Come again?"

"A program designed to increase a young child's brain activity." She clicked off the television. "They have research to show that it works."

His brows rose. "I still hear music."

She felt color creep into her cheeks. "I play a Mozart disc as he falls asleep." She walked past him to the kitchen and pulled two plates from a cabinet.

"Are you a classical-music fan?"

She spun around and stalked back to the table. "Why? Do you think classical is too highbrow for someone like me? Would it make more sense if I was a Toby Keith groupie?"

He took a step back and studied her. "First off, don't hate on Toby Keith. Secondly, it was a question." He waved one hand in the direction of the bookcases that flanked the television. "You have more classical CDs on your shelves than I've seen in my entire life. It's a logical assumption."

"Sorry." She sighed. "I like some composers but it's mainly for Charlie. I figure he needs all the help he can get, living with me. You may have heard I'm not the sharpest knife in the drawer."

"Is that so?"

"It's a well-known fact in town. My mom will tell you I have 'street smarts.'" She met his gaze with a wry smile. "I'm sure any number of my former friends would be happy to tell you how I skated through school by charming teachers or bullying other students into helping me." She broke off as Sam watched her, worrying that she'd somehow given him a clue into her defective inner self. She plastered on a saucy smile and stretched up her arms in an exaggerated pose. "At that point my life's ambition was to be a supermodel."

"Personally, I wanted to be Eddie Van Halen." He shrugged. "Were you really a bully?"

"I like to remember it as a benevolent dictatorship. I had my reasons, but have discovered that the kids I ordered around back in the day have become adults who are more than happy to see the golden girl taken down a few pegs." She opened the pizza box and pulled out a slice, embarrassed at her silly adolescent dream. "I was the ring leader and the 'pretty one' in Brevia, but couldn't cut it in the big leagues."

"You started over. There's nothing wrong with that. People do it all the time."

"Right. I went to beauty school, dated a string of losers, partied too much and tried to live below my potential." She tipped her beer in a mock toast. "And that's pretty low."

"Somebody did a number on you, sweetheart. Because

the way you handled that mess at the salon today took some clever negotiation skills. Not the work of a fool."

"We'll see what Val thinks once Ida spins it." She slid a piece of pizza onto his plate. "Sit down and eat. Unless the pizza was a ruse to get in the door so you could rip my head off without the neighbors hearing. Might be easier than going through with your *grand proposal.*"

His knee brushed against her bare leg as he folded himself into the chair across from her. It occurred to Julia that she was wearing only boxer shorts and a faded Red Hot Chili Peppers T-shirt with no bra. Bad choice for tonight.

"Such violent thoughts," he said, sprinkling a packet of cheese flakes on his pizza.

She sat back and crossed her arms over her chest. As soon as she'd realized she was braless, her nipples had sprung to attention as if to yell "over here, look at us." Not something she wanted Sam to notice in a million years.

"Why did you do it? This crazy situation is your fault."

He frowned. "You weren't exactly convincing as the levelheaded, responsible parent. You were about to dive across the table and take out the grandma."

"She deserved it." Julia popped out of her chair and grabbed a fleece sweatshirt from a hook near the hallway, trying not to let her belly show as she pulled it over her head. "But I didn't need to be rescued. Especially not by Three Strikes Sam." She sat back in her chair and picked up the pizza. "We're quite a pair. Do you really think anyone is going to believe you're engaged, given your reputation?"

"What reputation, and who is Three Strikes Sam?"

She finished her bite. "You don't know? Brevia is a small town. But we've got more than our share of single ladies. Apparently the long line of women you've dated since you arrived has banded together. The story is that you don't go on more than three dates with one woman. You've got your own fan club here in town. The ladies blog, tweet and keep track of you on Facebook. They call you Three Strikes Sam."

Sam felt as though he'd been kneed in the family jewels. Never mind the social-media insanity, what shocked him more was that Julia acted as if she knew the details of his dating history. That possibility was fright-night scary.

"You're making it up."

"I'm not that creative. You can log on to my computer and see for yourself. I only found out a couple of weeks ago, when Jean Hawkins was in the salon."

Sam swallowed hard. Jean was the dispatcher for the county sheriff's office. They'd had a couple of casual dinners last month but had agreed not to take it further. Or so he'd thought.

"She got a blowout and a bang trim. A 'wash that man right out of her hair' afternoon." Julia wrinkled her pert nose. "You know how it is—stylists are like therapists for some people. Get a woman in the chair and she has to spill her secrets."

"And *she* told you about this fan club?"

Julia nodded and took a drink of beer. "Three seems to be the magic number for you. You're a serial get-to-know-you dater."

Sam pushed away from the table and paced to the end of the narrow living room. "That's ridiculous." He ran a hand through his hair. "There's no arbitrary limit on the number of dates I'll go on with one woman."

"A dozen ladies claim there is," she countered. "They say you've more than made the rounds."

"I haven't dated a *dozen* ladies in Brevia. Besides, why would anyone gossip about dating me?"

"You've been in Brevia long enough to know how it

works." She laughed, but he found no humor in the situation. Sure, he'd been on dates with a few different women. When he'd first come to town, it had sort of happened that way. He'd always been a gentleman. If things led to the bedroom he didn't complain, but he also didn't push it. No one had grumbled at the time.

He wasn't a serial dater. The way she said it made him sound like a scumbag. So what if he was a little gun-shy? Walking in on your fiancée with her legs wrapped around another guy would do that to a man. It had been almost three years now since he'd had his heart crushed, and he wasn't itching to repeat that particular form of hell. "You're telling me I'm a joke with these women because I'm not in a relationship?" His voice started to rise. "In case they haven't noticed, I have a serious job. One that's more important to me than my damned social life."

"It's not like that," she said quickly, reaching out to place her cool fingers on his arm. A light touch that was oddly comforting. "No one is laughing at you. It's more like a challenge. Scary as it may sound, you have a town full of women who are determined to see you settle down. According to my sources, you're quite the catch."

He dropped back into the chair. "I came to Brevia because I wanted a fresh start."

"As Mick Jagger would say, 'you can't always get what you want.'"

"You think this fake engagement is what I need?"

"It was your idea to start. Plus, it's quieted the gossips, and your dad seemed to approve."

He nodded and took a long drink of beer. "My father loved you."

"Who can blame him?" she asked with a hair toss.

Sam smiled despite himself. "He wants to help me tap into my emotions."

She studied him as she took another bite. "Is that so bad?"

"I don't need to be more emotional."

"Your fans beg to differ."

"Don't remind me," he muttered.

A tiny cry came from the corner of the table and Julia adjusted a baby monitor. "I'm going to check on him." She padded down the hall, leaving Sam alone with his thoughts. Something he didn't need right now.

He preferred his emotions tightly bottled. It wasn't as if he didn't have feelings. Hell, he'd felt awful after calling off his engagement. He would have made a decent husband: loyal, faithful…

Maybe those were better attributes in a family pet, but he managed okay.

In Sam's opinion, there was no use wearing his heart on his sleeve. The scraps of memory he had from the months after his mother died were awful, his dad too often passed out drunk on the couch. Neighbors shuttling Sam and his brother to school and a steady diet of peanut butter and jelly sandwiches. When Joe finally got a handle on his emotions, it had saved their family.

Sam would never risk caring for someone like that. Feeling too much, connecting to the feelings he'd locked up tight, might spiral him back into that uncontrolled chaos.

He looked around the apartment, taking in more details with Julia out of the room. The dining area opened directly onto the living room, which was filled with comfortable, oversized furniture covered in a creamy fabric. Several fuzzy blankets fell over the arm of one chair. A wicker box overflowed with various toys, most of which looked far more complex than he remembered from childhood.

In addition to the classical CDs, framed pictures of Charlie with Julia, Vera, Lainey and Ethan sat on the bookshelves. Sam had also noticed an impressive collection of books—several classics by Hemingway, Dickens, even Ayn Rand. For someone who clearly didn't see her own intelligence, Julia had sophisticated taste in reading material.

The baby monitor crackled, drawing his attention. He heard Julia's voice through the static. "Did you have a dream, Charlie-boy?" she cooed. "Can Mommy sing you back to sleep?"

Charlie gave another sleepy cry as an answer and a moment later Sam heard a familiar James Taylor song in a soft soprano.

He smiled as he listened to Julia sing. Classical for Charlie, Sweet Baby James for his mother.

Sam felt a thread of unfamiliar connection fill his heart. At the same time there was a release of pressure he hadn't realized he'd held. In the quiet of the moment, listening to her sweet and slightly off-key voice, the day's stress slipped away. He took a deep breath as his shoulders relaxed.

"I love you, sweetie," he heard her whisper, her tone so full of tenderness it made his heart ache all the more.

He understood in an instant how much it meant for Julia to keep her son. Knew that she'd do anything to keep Charlie safe.

Suddenly Sam wanted that for her more than he cared about his own future. But he was a man who'd made it through life taking care of himself, protecting number one at all costs. No matter how he felt about one spirited single mother, he couldn't afford to change that now.

Hearing footsteps, he quickly stood to clear the dishes from the table.

"I think he's back down," she said as she came into the kitchen.

Sam rounded on her, needing to get to the crux of the matter before he completely lost control. "You're right," he told her. "This deal was my idea and I'll play the part of doting fiancé because it helps us both."

"Doting may be pushing it," she said, fumbling with the pizza box, clearly wary of his change in mood. "We don't need to go overboard."

He propped one hip on the counter. "We need to make it believable." He kept his tone all business. "Whatever it takes."

"Fine. We'll make people believe we're totally in love. I'm in. Whatever it takes to convince Jeff to drop the custody suit."

"Will he?"

"He still hasn't even seen Charlie. I get the impression his parents are pushing for the new custody deal. The attorney is really here to figure out if they have a viable case or not before they go public. Jeff didn't want kids in the first place. He'd even talked about getting the big snip. They probably think Charlie is their only shot at a grandchild, someone to mold and shape in their likeness."

"I don't think that's how kids work."

She shook her head. "I don't think they care. If we can convince Lexi that Charlie has a happy, stable home and that he's better off here than with Jeff and his family, that's the report she'll give to them. It will be enough. It has to. Once I get the custody agreement—"

"You'll dump my sorry butt," Sam supplied.

"Or you can break it off with me." She rinsed a plate and put it into the dishwasher. "People will expect it. You're up for reappointment soon. It should earn extra points with some of the council members. Everyone around here knows I'm a bad bet."

"I thought you and Ethan had been the town's golden couple back in the day."

"He was the golden boy," she corrected. "I was the eye

candy on his arm. But I messed that up. My first in a series of epic fails in the relationship department."

"Does it bother you that he's with Lainey?" Sam asked, not willing to admit how much her answer meant to him.

She smiled. "They're perfect together in a way he and I never were. She completes him and all that."

"Do you think there's someone out there who'd complete you?"

"Absolutely." She nodded. "At this moment, he's drooling in the crib at the end of the hall."

He took a step closer to her and tucked a lock of hair behind her ear. "We're going to make sure he stays there."

Her lips parted as she looked up at him. Instinctively he eased toward her.

She blinked and raised her hands to his chest, almost pushing him away but not quite. "We have to establish some ground rules," she said, sounding as breathless as he felt.

"I'm the law around these parts, ma'am," he said in his best Southern drawl. "I make the rules."

"Nice try." She laughed and a thrill ran through him. "First off, no touching or kissing of any kind."

It was his turn to throw back his head and laugh. "We're supposed to be in love. You think people will believe you could keep your hands off me?"

She smacked his chest lightly. "I'm surprised your ego made it through the front door. Okay, if the situation calls for it you can kiss me. A little." Her eyes narrowed. "But no tongue."

He tried to keep a straight face. "Where's the fun in that?"

"My best offer," she whispered.

He traced her lips with the tip of one finger and felt

himself grow heavy when they parted again. "I think we'd better practice to see if I'll be able to manage it."

He leaned in, but instead of claiming her mouth he tilted his head to reach the smooth column of her neck. He trailed delicate kisses up to her ear and was rewarded with a soft moan. Pushing her hair back, he cradled her face between his palms.

Her breath tingled against his skin and she looked at him, desire and self-control warring in the depths of her eyes. He wanted to keep this arrangement business but couldn't stop his overwhelming need. As out of control as a runaway train, he captured her lips with his.

Chapter Four

It should be illegal for a kiss to feel so good. The thought registered in Julia's dizzy brain. Followed quickly by her body's silent demand for more…more…more. Her arms wound around Sam's neck and she pressed into him, the heat from his body stoking a fire deep within her. His mouth melded to hers as he drew his hands up underneath her shirt.

A man hadn't kissed her like this in so long. As though he meant it, his mouth a promise of so much more.

A familiar voice cut through her lust-filled haze. "So, the rumors are true. Doesn't seem right your mother should be the last to know."

Sam's eyes flew open as he stepped away from her. Julia let out a soft groan.

"Ever think of knocking?" she asked, pressing her hands over her eyes.

"No" was her mother's succinct answer.

"Nice to see you, Mrs. Morgan." Although Sam's voice sounded a little shaky, Julia had to admire his courage in holding her mother's gaze.

Almost unwillingly, Julia turned and met her mom's steely glare. "I'm sorry, Mom. We wanted to keep things quiet a bit longer."

Vera Morgan was a tiny blonde dynamo of a woman. Her hair pulled back into a neat bun, she retained the beauty of her youth mixed with the maturity of decades spent overseeing her life and everyone in it. She crossed her arms over her chest. "Until you could announce your engagement in the middle of a crowded restaurant?"

Julia cringed. "Not the exact plan."

"I don't understand what this is about. It sounds like one of your typical impetuous decisions. Your father and I raised you to be more careful with how you act. I thought you'd have learned to be more responsible about the choices you make. Have you thought of Charlie? What's best for him?"

"He's all I think about and of course I want what's best for him. You have no idea..." Julia wanted to lay it all on the line for her mother—Jeff's family, the attorney, her fear of losing Charlie. She paused and glanced at Sam. He nodded slightly as if to encourage her.

How could she admit her years of bad choices could jeopardize Charlie's future? She knew her mother thought she was irresponsible, fickle and flighty. For most of her life, Julia had been all of those things and worse.

Her mother waited for an answer while the toe of one shoe tapped out a disapproving rhythm. Julia could measure the milestone moments of her life by her mother's slow toe tap. She swore sometimes she could hear it in her sleep.

"I don't expect you to understand, but this is good for Charlie. For both of us."

Vera's gaze slanted between Julia and Sam. "Having the hots for a guy isn't the same as love. From what I just witnessed, you two have chemistry, but marriage is a lot more than physical attraction."

Julia felt a blush rise to her cheeks. "I'm not a teenager anymore," she mumbled. "I get that."

"I worry about you rushing into something." Vera paused and pinned Sam with a look before continuing. "Especially with a man who has a reputation around town. I don't want you to be hurt."

"I know what I'm doing. Trust me. For once trust that I'm making the right decision." She hated that her voice cracked. She'd made some stupid choices in her life. So what? Lots of people did and they lived through it. Did she have to be raked over the coals for every indiscretion?

Sam's hand pressed into the small of her back, surprisingly comforting. "Mrs. Morgan," he began, his voice strong and confident. Julia wished she felt either right now. "Your daughter is the most amazing woman I've ever met."

Julia glanced over her shoulder, for a moment wondering if he was talking about her sister.

The corner of his mouth turned up as he looked at her. "*You* are amazing. You're honest and brave and willing to fight for what you want."

Charlie's sweet face flashed in Julia's mind, and she gave a slight nod.

"You're a lot stronger and smarter than you give yourself credit for." His gaze switched to Vera. "Than most people give her credit for. But that's going to change. I want people to see the woman I do. Maybe we shouldn't have hidden our relationship, but it wasn't anyone's business. To hell with my reputation and Julia's, too."

"I hear a couple town-council members are making a big deal about your single status as they're starting to review your contract. They think only a family man can impart the kind of values and leadership Brevia needs."

"Another reason we were quiet. I don't want to use Julia and Charlie to get reappointed. The job I've done as police chief should be enough."

He sounded so convincing, Julia almost believed him. At the very least, his conviction gave her the courage to stand up for herself a little more. "Sam's right. We're not looking for anyone's approval. This is about us."

"Have you set a date yet?" Vera asked, her tone hard again.

"We're working on that."

Sam cleared his throat. "I'm going to head home." He dropped a quick kiss on Julia's cheek. "I'll talk to you tomorrow."

"Coward," she whispered.

"Sticks and stones," he said softly before turning to Vera.

"Mrs. Morgan, I'm sorry you found out this way. I hope you know I have Julia and Charlie's best interests at heart."

Her mother's eyes narrowed.

"That's my cue." Sam scooted around Vera and let himself out the front door.

"I only want what's best for you." Vera stepped forward. "Your father and I didn't do enough to help you when you were younger. I won't make that mistake again." She wrapped one arm around Julia's waist. "I don't understand how this happened and I don't trust Sam Callahan. But I know Charlie is your number one priority. That's what counts."

Julia didn't want her mother to feel guilty. As a child, she'd tried to hide the extent of her problems from her parents, as well as everyone else. They weren't to blame. She let out a slow breath. "I'm doing this for Charlie."

"You love him?"

"He's my entire life."

"I meant, do you love Sam? Enough to marry him."

"Sam is a wonderful man," Julia answered quickly. "I'd be a fool not to want to marry him." Not exactly a declaration of deep and abiding love but it was as much as she could offer tonight. "I'm sorry you had to come over."

Her mother watched her for several moments before releasing her hold. "You're my daughter. I'll do anything to protect you. You know that, right?"

Julia nodded. Once again, she had the urge to share the whole sordid mess with her mother. She swallowed back her emotions. "It's late. I'll bring Charlie by in the morning before I drop him at the sitter's."

Vera patted her cheek. "Get some sleep. You look like you could use it. You can't keep up this pace. You're no spring chicken."

"Thanks for the reminder." That was the reason Julia wanted to handle this on her own. Vera couldn't help but judge her. It was in her mother's nature to point out all the ways Julia needed improvement. She'd have a field day with the custody situation. Julia had enough trouble without adding her mother's opinion into the mix.

She closed and locked the door behind her mother then sagged against it. She'd done a lot of reckless things in her life but wondered if this time she'd gone off the deep end.

The baby monitor made a noise. Charlie gave a short cry before silence descended once more. Her gaze caught on a framed photo on one end table, taken minutes after his birth. She'd known as soon as the nurse had placed him in her arms that Charlie was the best part of her. She'd vowed that day to make something of her life, to become worthy of the gift she'd been given. While she had a difficult time tamping down her self-doubt, she never questioned how far she would go to protect her son. She'd do whatever it took to keep him safe, even this ridiculous charade with Sam. If it helped her custody case in the least, Julia would become the most devoted fiancée Brevia had ever seen.

That commitment was put to the test the next morning when a posse of angry women descended on the salon. Two to be exact, but it felt like a mob.

She'd swung by her mother's after breakfast then dropped Charlie with Mavis Donnelly, the older woman who watched him and one other toddler in her home. She'd gotten into town by eight-thirty, thanks to Charlie's propensity to wake with the sun. She wanted time to look over the monthly billing spreadsheets before anyone else arrived.

No one outside her immediate family knew about her condition, and she intended to keep it that way, afraid of being taken advantage of or thought too stupid to handle her own business. She put in the extra time she needed to get each financial piece right. Sometimes she studied the numbers until she felt almost physically ill.

When the knocking started, she straightened from her desk in the back, assuming it was one of the stylists who'd forgotten her key. Instead the front door swung open to reveal two pairs of angry eyes glaring at her.

"How'd you do it?" Annabeth Sullivan asked, pushing past her into the salon without an invitation. Annabeth had been in the same high-school class as Julia, a girl Julia would have referred to as a "band geek" back in the day. She hadn't been kind, and Annabeth, who now managed the bank reviewing Julia's loan application, hadn't let her forget it. Annabeth's younger sister, Diane, followed her inside.

"Morning to you, ladies."

"He never goes on more than three dates." Annabeth held up three plump fingers. "Never."

"Can I see the ring?" Diane asked, her tone gentler.

Reluctantly, Julia held out her hand. "It's perfect," Diane gushed.

"Kind of small," Annabeth said, peering at it from the corner of one eye. "I figured you'd go for the gaudy flash."

Julia felt her temper flare. "You don't know me, then."

Annabeth took a step closer. "I know you, Julia Morgan. I know you had your minions stuff my locker with Twinkies the first day of freshman year. And made my life hell every day after that. I spent four years trying to stay off your radar and still you'd hunt me down."

The truth of the accusation made Julia cringe. "I'm sorry. I tried to make amends when I came back. I was awful and I'm truly sorry. I offered you free services for a year to try to repay a tiny portion of my debt."

"A year?" Diane turned to her sister. "You never told me that."

"Be quiet, Diane. That doesn't matter now. What I want to know is how you cast your evil spell over Sam Callahan."

"I'm not a witch. No spells, no magic." She paused then added, "We fell in love. Simple enough. Is there something else you need?" She took a step toward the front door but Annabeth held up a hand.

"Nothing is simple with you. Sam is a good man. He went on three dates with Diane."

"Almost four," Diane added. "I thought I'd made it past the cutoff. But he got called to a fire and had to cancel our last dinner. After that, he told me he wanted to be just friends."

"So, how come you two are all of a sudden engaged when no one even knew you were dating?"

"Even Abby was surprised and she knows *everything* about Sam." Diane clamped a hand over her mouth as Annabeth leveled a scowl at her.

As Julia understood it, Abby Brighton had moved to Brevia to take care of her elderly grandfather. She was the police chief's secretary and dispatcher. She didn't know about Abby's relationship with Sam, but the way Annabeth was looking at her sister, there was more to the story.

"Plus, you're a little long in the tooth for Sam," Annabeth stated, getting back to the business at hand.

Her mom had just said she was no spring chicken and now this. Lucky thing she'd chucked her ego to the curb years ago. "I'm thirty-two, the same age as you, Annabeth. We're not quite over the hill."

Annabeth pulled a small notebook out of her purse. "That's old for Sam. He usually dates women at least four years younger than him."

"And how old is that?"

"Don't you know how old he is?" Diane asked.

Julia met Annabeth's shrewd gaze. Calculated error on her part. "Of course. What I don't understand is why you carry a notebook with Sam's dating stats in it."

Annabeth snapped the notebook shut. "I don't have his dating stats, just a few pertinent facts. He and Diane seemed closer than any of the other women he dated. I want my sister to be happy. She had a chance before you came into the picture."

Julia studied Diane and couldn't begin to picture the dainty woman and Sam as a couple. "Did Sam break your heart?"

Diane scrunched up her nose. "No," she admitted after a moment. "Don't get me wrong, he's supercute and such a gentleman. But he's a little um...big...for me."

Julia's mouth dropped open. "Big?"

"Not like that," Diane amended. "He's just…with the uniform, all those muscles and he's so tall. It's kind of intimidating."

"I know what you mean," Julia agreed, although Sam's size appealed to her. She was five-nine, so it took a lot of guy to make Julia feel petite, but Sam did it in a way that also made her feel safe.

"You have real feelings for him." Annabeth interrupted her musings.

"I… We're engaged. I'd better have real feelings."

"Frankly, I thought this was another one of your stunts to show up the other single women in town. Prove that you're still the leader of the pack and all that." She glanced at Diane. "I didn't want my sister to fall prey to you the way I did."

"I'm *not* the same person I was. I can apologize but you'll need to choose whether to forgive me. I don't blame you if the answer is no, but it's your decision. My priority is Charlie. I want to live a life that will make him proud. I don't intend to re-create the past. You're married now, right?"

The other woman nodded. "Five years to my college sweetheart. He's my best friend."

"Why is it so strange to believe that I might want that for myself? My parents had a great marriage and you probably remember my sister recently married the love of her life, who just happened to be *my* high-school sweetheart. They're happy and I want to be happy. Last time I checked, that wasn't a crime in this town."

Julia pointed a finger at Diane. "If your sister wants to find a man, she will without you hunting down potential suitors for her or tallying lists of how far ahead of other women she is in the dating pool. Sam is a real person, too. I don't think he intended to become such a hot topic of gossip. He's living his life the best way he can. We both are." She stopped for breath and noticed Annabeth and Diane staring at her, eyebrows raised.

She realized how much she'd revealed with her little tirade and tried to calm her panic. Maybe she didn't want to be known as the town's head mean girl anymore, but she had a reputation to protect. She made people think she didn't take things seriously so that they'd never notice when she got hurt. She plastered a smile on her face. "What? Was that a little too mama grizzly for you?"

Annabeth shook her head, looking dazed. "I didn't realize that's how you felt about things. Sam is lucky to have you."

"I'm not sure—"

"I'm sure."

The three women turned to see Sam standing in the doorway. Julia's face burned. "How much did you hear?"

"Enough to know that I agree with Annabeth. I'm damned lucky to have you."

Annabeth and Diane scooted toward the front door. "If you'll excuse us. We'll leave you two alone."

He didn't move. "Is this going to hit the gossip train or however it works?"

Diane shook her head. "We weren't the ones who started analyzing you. It was—"

Annabeth gave her sister a hard pinch on the arm. "It doesn't matter anymore. It's clear you're not the person everyone thought."

Sam eased to the side of the doorway. "I think that could be said for more than just me."

Annabeth threw a glance at Julia and nodded.

"Maybe you should spread that news around."

"I'll get on it, Chief." The two women hurried out of the salon, and Sam pulled the door shut behind them.

"I'm a real man?" he said, repeating Julia's earlier comment. "I'm glad you think so, Ms. Morgan."

Julia slumped into a chair, breathing as if she'd just finished a marathon run. Her eyes were bleak as they met his. "It's pointless, Sam. This is never going to work."

Chapter Five

Sam stared at Julia. Her blond hair curled around her shoulders and fell forward, covering one high cheekbone. His fingers itched to smooth it back from her face, to touch her skin and wipe the pain from those large gray eyes. She looked so alone sitting in the oversized stylist's chair.

Sam knew what it felt like to be alone. Hell, he'd courted solitude for most of his life. He'd learned early on only to depend on himself, because when he relied on other people for his happiness he got hurt. First when his mother died and his dad had almost lost it. Then, later, in the relationship that had ended with his fiancée cheating on him.

He'd come to believe that happiness was overrated. He wanted to work hard and make a difference—the only way he knew to chase the demons away for a little peace.

When he'd heard Julia defending his character, something tight in his gut unwound. He was used to making things happen and having people depend on him. He prided himself on not needing anyone. It bothered him to know that women were spreading rumors about him, but he would have soldiered through with his head held high. Hearing Julia take on those ladies had made him realize he liked not feeling totally alone.

Her declaration that they couldn't make it work made no sense. "Why the change of heart?" He moved closer to her. "You convinced Annabeth and Diane."

"How old are you?"

"Thirty-three."

"Why do you only date younger women?"

He stopped short. "I don't."

"Are you sure? I've heard you average women at least four years younger. I'm thirty-two. My birthday's in two months."

"I don't ask a woman about her age before we go out. If there's a connection, that's what I go on."

"You never asked me out."

"I asked you to marry me," he said, blowing out a frustrated breath. "Doesn't that count?"

She shook her head. "I mean when you first came to town. When you were making the rounds."

"I didn't make the rounds. Besides, you were pregnant."

"I haven't been pregnant for a while."

"Did you want me to ask you out?" The attraction he'd denied since the first time he saw her roared to life again.

She shook her head again. "I'm just curious, like most of the town is now. We've barely spoken to each other in the last two years."

"I thought the idea was that we were keeping the relationship under wraps."

"What's your favorite color?"

"Green," he answered automatically then held up a hand. "What's going on? I don't understand why you think this won't work. You made a believer of Annabeth Sullivan, the town's main gossip funnel."

Julia stood and glanced at her watch. "The girls will start coming in any minute. I don't know, Sam. This is complicated."

"Only if you make it complicated."

"What's my favorite food?"

"How the heck am I supposed to know?"

"If we were in love, you'd know."

Sam thought about his ex-fiancée and tried to conjure a memory of what she'd like to eat. "Salad?" he guessed.

Julia rolled her eyes. "Nobody's favorite food is salad. Mine is lobster bisque."

Sam tapped one finger on the side of his head. "Got it."

"There's more to it than that."

"Come to dinner tonight," he countered.

"Where?"

"My place. Five-thirty. I talked to my dad this morning. He didn't mention delving into my emotions once. Huge progress as far as I'm concerned. He can't wait to spend more time with you."

"That's a bad idea, and I have Charlie."

"The invitation is for both of you." He took her shoulders between his hands. "We're going to make this work, Julia. Bring your list of questions tonight—favorite color, food, movie, whatever."

"There's more to it than—"

"I know but it's going to work." As if by their own accord, his fingers strayed to her hair and he sifted the golden strands between them. "For both of us."

At the sound of voices in the salon, Julia's back stiffened and her eyes widened a fraction. "You need to go."

"We're engaged," he reminded her. "We want people to see us together."

"Not here."

He wanted to question her but she looked so panicked, he decided to give her a break. "Dinner tonight," he repeated, and as three women emerged from the hallway behind the salon's main room, he bent forward and pressed his lips against hers.

Her sharp intake of breath made him smile. "Lasagna," he whispered against her mouth.

"What?" she said, her voice as dazed as he felt.

"My favorite food is lasagna."

She nodded and he kissed her again. "See you later, sweetheart," he said and pulled back, leaving Julia and the three stylists staring at him.

"Abby, how old are you?" Sam stepped out of his office into the lobby of the police station.

Abby Brighton, who'd started as the receptionist shortly after he'd been hired, looked up from her computer. "I'll be twenty-eight in the fall."

"That's young."

"Not really," she answered. "Maggie Betric is twenty-six and Suzanne over at the courthouse in Jefferson just turned twenty-five."

"Twenty-five?" Sam swallowed. He'd gone out to dinner with both women and had no idea they'd been that much younger than him. When did he become a small-town cradle robber? Jeez. He needed to watch himself.

"Julia's in her thirties, right?" Abby asked.

"Thirty-two."

"When's her birthday?"

"Uh…" Wait, he knew this. "It's in May."

Abby turned her chair around to face him. "I still can't believe I didn't know you two were dating."

"No one knew."

"But I know everything about you." She looked away. "Not everything, of course. But a lot. Because I make the schedule and we work so closely together."

He studied Abby another minute. She was cute, in a girl-next-door sort of way. Her short pixie cut framed a small face, her dark eyes as big as saucers. They'd worked together for almost two years now, and he supposed she did know him better than most people. But what did he know about her? What did he know about anyone, outside his dad and brother?

Sure, Sam had friends, a Friday-night poker game, fishing with the boys. He knew who was married and which guys were confirmed bachelors. Did knowing the kind of beer his buddies drank count as being close?

"Do you have a boyfriend, Abby?"

Her eyes widened farther. "Not at the moment."

"And your only family in town is your granddad?"

She nodded.

Okay, that was good. He knew something about the woman he saw every day at work. He looked around her brightly colored workspace. "I'm guessing your favorite color is yellow."

She smiled. "Yours is hunter green."

How did she know that?

"Does Julia make you happy?" she asked after a moment.

"Yes," he answered automatically. "Why?"

"I just wouldn't have pictured her as your type." Abby fidgeted with a paper clip. "She's beautiful and everything, but I always saw you with someone more…"

"More?"

"Someone nicer, I suppose."

"You don't think Julia's nice? Has she been unkind to you?"

Abby shook her head. "No, but I hear stories from when she was in high school. I'm in a book club with some ladies who knew her then."

"People change."

"You deserve someone who will take care of you."

"I'm a grown man, Abby. I can take care of myself."

"I know but you need—" She stopped midsentence when the phone rang. She answered and, after a moment, cupped her hand over the receiver. "Someone ran into a telephone pole out at the county line. No injuries but a live wire might be down."

Sam nodded and headed for the front door. "Call it in to the utility company. I'm on my way."

He drove toward the edge of town, grateful to get out and clear his head. He'd done more talking about himself and what he needed and felt in the past twenty-four hours than he had in the previous five years. His dad's fault, for sure.

This engagement was supposed to help Sam dodge his father's attempts to make him more in touch with his feelings. Hopefully, this dinner would smooth things over enough so life could return to normal. Other than the pretend engagement.

It wouldn't be as difficult as Julia thought to fool people. They'd hold hands, be seen around town together for a few PDAs and everyone would believe them. Kissing Julia was one of the perks of this arrangement. He loved her moment of surprise each time he leaned in. Sam hadn't been with a woman for a long time, which must explain why her touch affected him so much.

He understood the importance of making this work. Tonight, they'd come to an understanding of how to get what they both wanted.

* * *

Julia lifted Charlie out of his car seat and turned to face the quaint house tucked onto one of the tree-lined streets near downtown Brevia.

"He even has a picket fence," she said to her son, who answered her with a hearty laugh and a slew of indecipherable words.

"My sentiments exactly." She kissed the top of Charlie's head.

"Do you need a hand?"

Joe Callahan stepped off the porch and headed toward her.

"I've got it, Mr. Callahan. Thank you."

He met her halfway up the walk. "Call me Joe. And you—" he held out his hands for Charlie "—can call me Papa."

"Pap-y," Charlie repeated in his singsong voice and leaned forward for Joe to scoop him up. Her son, the extrovert.

"You don't have to do that."

Joe was already swinging Charlie above his head, much to the boy's delight. "What a handsome fellow," he said. He smiled at Julia. "He favors his beautiful mother."

Julia couldn't help but return his grin. "Are you always this charming?"

Joe gave an easy laugh. "For decades I was a real hard—" He lifted Charlie again. "I was hard-nosed. A walking grim reaper. Sam and his brother got the brunt of that. I've learned a lot since then."

"Wisdom you want to impart to your son?"

"If he'll let me." Joe tucked Charlie into the crook of his arm and the boy shoved his fist into his mouth, sucking contently. "You've already helped him start."

It was Julia's turn to laugh. "I don't have much wisdom to share with anyone."

Joe started toward the house. "Mothers have inherent wisdom. My late wife was the smartest, most insightful woman I've ever met."

"How old was Sam when she died?"

"Ten and Scott was seven. It was a dark period for our family."

"Was it a long illness?"

Joe turned and immediately Julia realized her mistake. "Sam hasn't told you about his mother?"

She shook her head, unable to hide her lack of knowledge. "It's difficult for him to speak about."

Joe sighed as if he understood. "That's my fault. After Lorraine passed, I was so overcome with grief that I shut down and made the boys do the same. Looking back, it was selfish and cowardly. They were kids and they needed me."

Julia patted his arm. "How did she die?"

"A car accident," he said quietly. Charlie rested his small head on Joe's shoulder as if sensing the older man needed comfort.

"How tragic. I'm so sorry for all of you."

"The tragic part was that it was my fault. I'd been on the force over ten years. I became obsessed with being the most dedicated cop Boston had ever seen. Like a bonehead, I took on the most dangerous assignments they'd give me—whatever I could do to prove that I was the baddest dude on the block. Lorraine couldn't handle the stress. She begged me to slow down. I wouldn't listen, brushed aside her worries and only focused on what I wanted."

He ran his hands through his hair, so much like Sam, then continued, "She'd started drinking at night—not so much that she was falling-down drunk, but enough to numb her. I was tuned out and didn't realize how bad it had gotten. I got home late one night and we fought. She went for a drive after the boys were in bed—to cool off. She wasn't even a half mile from the house when she ran the red light. She swerved to avoid another car. Wrapped her car around a telephone pole. She was gone instantly."

Julia sucked in a breath. The first time she'd met Sam had been when he'd found her after she'd hydroplaned on a wet road and gone over an embankment, her car slamming into a tree. She'd been pregnant at the time, and thinking the accident might have hurt her baby had been the scariest moment of her life. Sam had gotten her to the hospital and stayed with her until Lainey had arrived. She wondered if he'd thought about his mother during that time, or if it had just been another day on the job.

"How devastating for all of you." She leaned forward and wrapped her arms around Joe. Charlie squealed with delight then wriggled to be let down.

"Okay." She lifted him from Joe's arms and deposited him on the porch.

Joe swiped at his eyes. "I would have followed her in a minute. I could barely function and had two boys at home who needed me more than ever. Instead, I threw myself into the job like I was tempting fate. If they gave awards for stupidity and selfishness, I would have been a top candidate."

"Nothing can prepare you for something like that. I'm sure you did the best you could. Sam and his brother must know that."

Joe held open the screen door and Charlie headed into the house. "It should have been a wake-up call but it took me another twenty years to get my priorities straight. I want to make it right by Sam."

She looked into Joe Callahan's kind eyes and her stomach twisted. Julia didn't have much luck making things right by anyone, and if Joe knew the details of their arrangement, it would break his heart.

"Mama, come." Charlie peered around the doorway to the kitchen. Charlie. He was the reason she'd entered into this deal in the first place.

"Where's Sam?" She held out her hand to her son, who ran toward her to take it.

Joe smiled. "Grilling out back."

She scooped Charlie into her arms and followed Joe down the hall. She'd guess Sam's house had been built in the early 1900s, and he'd obviously renovated, drawing inspiration from the Craftsman tradition with hardwood floors throughout. In the open kitchen, beautiful maple cabinets hung on each wall. The colors were neutral but not boring, a mix of classic and modern traditions.

Joe led her through one of the French doors that opened to the back patio. It hadn't rained for a couple of days, and while it was cool, the evening air held the unmistakable scent of spring, with the elms and oaks surrounding the green yard beginning to bud.

Sam stood in front of a stainless-steel grill, enveloped in smoke. He turned and smiled at her and her chest caught again. He wore a dark T-shirt, faded jeans and flip-flops. Julia hadn't often seen him out of uniform, and while the casual outfit should have made him less intimidating, certain parts of her body responded differently.

"Ball," Charlie shouted and squirmed in her arms. When Julia put him down, he ran toward an oversized bouncy ball and several plastic trucks stacked near the wrought-iron table.

Sam closed the grill's lid and met her questioning gaze. "I thought he'd like some toys to play with over here."

She nodded, a little dumbfounded at the impact the small gesture had on her.

"Sammy said you two are mainly at your place."

"It's easier that way."

"Have you given any thought to where you'll live once you're married?"

"Here," Sam answered at the same time Julia said, "Not really."

Joe's brows furrowed, so she added, "My apartment is a rental, so I assumed we'd move in with Sam."

Sam came to her side and placed a quick kiss on her forehead. "We're going to make the spare bedroom into Charlie's room."

Julia coughed wildly.

"Can I get you a glass of water?" Sam asked.

"I'll grab it," Joe said and disappeared into the house.

Sam clapped her on the back. "Are you okay?"

"Not at all." She drew in a breath. "Charlie's room?"

"We're engaged, remember. It's going to seem strange enough that the kid barely knows me. I didn't have any of his stuff or toys in the house and my dad started asking questions."

At that moment, the bouncy ball knocked against Julia's leg.

"Ball, Mama. Ball." Charlie squealed with delight.

Sam handed Julia a pair of tongs. "Will you pull the steaks off the grill?" He picked up the ball and tucked it under his arm. "I'm going in for some male bonding."

Julia watched, fascinated as Sam walked over to Charlie and held out a hand. Without hesitation, Charlie took it and Sam led him into the yard to roll the ball back and forth.

The only man in Charlie's life was Ethan. Julia tried not to depend too much on him. Lainey, Ethan and Julia had a long history between them, and Julia didn't want to push the limits of their relationship.

Charlie did his best to mimic Sam's motions as he rolled

and threw the ball, and Julia realized how important it was for her son to have a father figure.

"I knew he'd be great with kids," Joe said as he handed her a tall glass of water. "Scott is a wild one, but Sam..."

"Why do you think Sam never married?" Julia asked, tapping one finger against her lips. Annabeth's story about Sam's record as a three-dates-and-done serial dater came back to her.

"It's not for lack of trying," Joe answered candidly then amended. "But I can tell you're a better fit for him than Jenny."

Julia tried not to look startled. "Jenny?"

Joe studied her. "His ex-fiancée. He *did* tell you about her?"

"He was really hurt when it ended," she offered, not an outright lie but enough to cover her lack of knowledge. She and Sam had a lot they needed to get clear about each other if this charade was going to work.

Joe nodded. "Not that he would have told anyone. He bottled up his emotions just like I'd done when his mom passed. But Jenny's infidelity was a huge blow to him."

"I can understand why." Julia's mind reeled at this new information. Sam had been previously engaged and his fiancée had cheated on him. That might explain a little about his commitment issues.

"She wasn't a good match even before that. Sure, she was perfect on paper—a schoolteacher, sweet and popular with his friends, but she didn't get him. They were marrying what they thought they wanted without paying attention to what they needed."

Julia understood that line of thinking better than most. It was what had led her to believe her ex-boyfriend could make her happy. She'd thought she loved Jeff but realized what she loved was the image she'd had of him, not who he truly was. Was that what Sam had thought about his ex, as well, or had this Jenny been the love of his life? The thought gave Julia a sick feeling in the pit of her stomach.

Sam looked up from where he was currently chasing Charlie across the backyard. "How about those steaks, sweetie?"

"I'm on it," she called and headed for the grill.

Much to Joe's delight, Charlie insisted on sitting on Sam's lap during dinner. Sam looked vaguely uncomfortable as the toddler fed him bites of meat but dutifully ate each one.

In addition to the steak, Sam had roasted vegetables and made a salad. She'd brought a loaf of bread from the bakery next to the salon, along with a bottle of red wine. The dinner was surprisingly fun and Julia found herself relaxing. Joe did most of the talking, regaling her with stories, of his years with the force and more recently of the workshops he facilitated around the region.

"Someone needs a diaper change," she said as they finished the meal. At the look of horror on Sam's face, she laughed. "I'll take it from here."

"Good idea," he agreed.

"You'd better get used to stinky bottoms," his father chided.

Sam's eyes widened and Julia laughed again. "All in good time, Joe. For now, I'll take the poop duty."

Sam stood quickly and handed Charlie to her. "I'll clear the dishes." To her surprise, he placed a soft kiss on her mouth. Charlie giggled and Julia felt her world tilt the tiniest bit.

"Right," she said around a gulp of air. She met Joe's gaze as she turned for the house and he winked at her. Right. Sam was her fake fiancé. Of course he was going to kiss her sometimes. They'd discussed that it was all part of the act. It didn't mean anything.

At least, not to her.

Right.

She changed Charlie's diaper on the floor of Sam's living room. Unlike her cozy apartment filled with well-worn flea-market finds and hand-me-downs from her mother, the furnishings in this room appeared very new and hardly used.

A sleek leather couch faced an entertainment center with an enormous flat-screen television and several pieces of stereo equipment. He had a few books scattered on the shelves, mainly fly-fishing manuals and guidebooks for the North Carolina mountains. A couple of pieces of abstract art hung on the walls. Unlike her family room, there wasn't a single framed photo of any of Sam's family or friends.

Julia loved the reminders of each stage in Charlie's life on display around her house. It was as though Sam didn't have a personal life. Maybe it was just a guy thing, she thought, but then remembered how Jeff had documented each of his research trips with photos spread around their condo in Columbus.

Maybe not.

She pulled on Charlie's sweatpants and watched as he scrambled to his feet and headed back toward the kitchen.

"Hey, little man, where are you headed in such a rush?"

Joe picked him up as Charlie answered, "Ou-side," and he planted a raspberry on the boy's belly, making him laugh out loud.

"I'll see you later, gator." Joe put Charlie on the ground and he made a beeline for the back of the house.

"It was nice to spend time with you." Julia gave the older man a quick hug.

"I hope it's the first of many dinners. I'd love to meet

your family while I'm in town. Sammy said your mom is famous around here for the animal shelter she runs."

"It was a labor of love after my dad died." The thought of Joe Callahan and her mother getting together made her want to squirm. Keeping their respective families separate would make the summer much simpler. The complications of this arrangement were almost more than she could handle.

"I meant what I said at the restaurant," Joe told her. "Sam will protect you and Charlie. I don't know the details of your custody arrangement, but I believe that boy is better off with you than anyone else in the world."

Julia blinked back sudden tears. "Thank you. I better go track him down."

Joe nodded. "Good night, Julia. I'll see you soon."

The front door shut behind him, and Julia thought about Joe's last words. Charlie was better off with her. She had to believe that. He belonged to her and she to him. Nothing and no one was going to change that.

She turned for the kitchen just as Charlie's high-pitched scream came from the backyard.

Chapter Six

Julia raced onto the patio, following the sounds of her son's cries, her heart pounding in her chest.

Sam stood in the backyard, cradling Charlie against his chest with one arm. With his free hand he waved the tongs she'd used for the meat. A large gray dog hopped up and down in front of him.

"What happened?" Julia yelled as she sprinted down the back steps. "Is Charlie hurt?"

At the sound of his mother's voice, the boy lifted his tear-streaked face from Sam's shoulder. "Ball, Mama. No doggy." He pointed a slobbery finger at the Weimaraner running circles in the yard, the deflated bouncy ball clamped in his jaws.

His eyes never leaving the dog, Sam scooted closer to Julia. "Charlie's fine. Take him back to the house. I've never seen this animal before. He could be rabid."

Charlie shook his head. "No doggy," he repeated. "Charlie ball."

Julia looked from her son to Sam to the dog bounding and leaping, his stubby tail wagging, clearly relishing this impromptu game of keep-away. Rabid? Overenthusiastic and in need of some training. Not rabid.

Julia had grown up with a variety of animals underfoot. Her dad had been Brevia's vet for years, and the shelter her mother had built and run after his death attracted animals from all over the South. Her mom's ability to rehabilitate strays was legendary—Vera had even written a dog-behavior book that had become a bestseller a few years ago. Julia might not be the expert her mother was, but she had a fairly good sense for reading canine energy. And every inch of the Weimaraner was shouting "let's play."

"Sam, the dog isn't going to hurt you."

"It bared its teeth. It's a lunatic."

"You've never seen it before?" Julia moved slowly forward.

"No. I told you to get back on the porch. I don't want you or Charlie hurt."

She gave a quick whistle. The dog stopped and looked at her, its tail still wagging.

"Julia, you can't—"

"Drop it," she commanded, her finger pointed to the ground.

"Dop." Charlie mimicked her. "Charlie ball."

The dog waited a moment then lowered the lump of plastic to the ground.

"Sit."

The dog's bottom plopped to the ground.

She held out her palm. "Stay."

She took a step toward the dog. His bottom lifted but she gave a stern "No," and he sank back down.

"I'm sorry about your ball, sweetie," she told Charlie.

"Bad," he said with a whine.

"Not bad, but he needs someone to help him learn."

As she got nearer, the animal trembled with excitement.

"You shouldn't be that close."

"Do you have any rope?"

"I'm not leaving you out here. I'm serious. Back off from the dog."

"What is your problem? This dog isn't a threat."

"You don't know—"

As if sensing that her attention was divided, the dog stood and bounded the few feet toward her. The skin around its mouth drew back and wrinkled, exposing a row of shiny teeth.

"Get back, Julia. It's snarling." Sam lunged forward, but before he got the animal, the dog flopped at Julia's feet and flipped onto his back, writhing in apparent ecstasy as she bent to rub his belly.

Sam stopped in his tracks. "What the…?"

"He's a smiler."

"Dogs don't smile."

"Some do."

Charlie wriggled out of Sam's arms and, before either of them could stop him, headed for the dog. "Good doggy. No ball."

Julia put an arm around Charlie, holding him back, as Sam's breath hitched. "You shouldn't let him so near that thing."

She offered what she hoped was a reassuring smile. "My mom runs an animal shelter, remember? Charlie's been around dogs since he was born. I'm careful to supervise him and make sure he's safe." She tickled her fingers under the dog's ear and got a soft lick on her arm for the effort. "This boy is gorgeous."

"A good-looking animal can still be crazy."

Julia's shoulders stiffened. "What makes you think he's crazy?" Before he'd left for good, Jeff had said something similar to her. He'd told her she was beautiful but a nut job. He'd thrown in a dig about her intelligence as icing on the cake.

Her mother was the expert on stray animals, but Julia knew a thing or two about being damaged on the inside. Her gut told her this dog had a heart of gold.

"He snarled at me."

"He *smiled* at you," she insisted. "Pet him. He's a real sweetie."

"I don't like dogs," Sam said simply.

"I wouldn't have guessed it." She ran her hand along the length of the dog's side. "He's way underweight. No collar and he's dirty. I'd guess he's been on his own for a while now. You haven't seen him around?"

Sam shook his head. "A section of the fenced yard came loose in the storm a few nights ago. He must have smelled the grill and come in that way."

She straightened. "Would you take Charlie for a minute? I have a leash in the trunk of my car."

"You don't have a dog."

"Mom makes everyone keep an extra in case we come across a stray." The Weimaraner jumped to his feet and nudged at Julia's pants leg.

"Mama doggy," Charlie said as Julia shifted him into Sam's arms.

"No, honey, not mine. We'll take him to Grandma in the morning and she'll find a good home for him."

Charlie frowned. "Mama doggy."

Julia noticed Sam tense as the dog trotted over to sniff him. "Are you scared of dogs, Chief Callahan?"

"Wary, not scared." He held Charlie a little higher in his arms.

"If you say so." She headed up the steps toward the house and the dog followed.

"What if he runs away?"

"I have a feeling he'll stick close by. Weims are usually Velcro dogs."

"Are you going to keep him overnight?"

She nodded. "It won't be the first time. Mom says the strays have a knack for finding me. The scrappier they are, the harder I work to bring them in. I've rescued dogs from Dumpsters, highway ditches—"

"Stop!" Sam shook his head. "The thought of you luring in unknown dogs from who knows where makes my head pound."

"What can I tell you?" She laughed. "I have a soft spot for lost causes."

Sam met her gaze then, and for an instant she saw the kind of longing and vulnerability in his eyes she'd never imagined from a man as tough and strong as he seemed. "Lucky dogs," he whispered.

The hair on her arms stood on end and her mouth went dry. He blinked, closing off his feelings from her.

"Add this one to the lucky list," she said, her voice a little breathy. Quickly, she led the dog through the house, grabbing a piece of bread off the counter for good measure. But she didn't need it. The dog walked by her side, his early rambunctiousness tempered because he had her attention.

She pulled the leash out of her trunk and looped it over his head. He shook his head, as if he wasn't used to a collar. "Easy there, boy," Julia crooned and knelt to pet him. The dog nuzzled into her chest. "I bet you've had a rough time of it. If anyone can find you a good home, it's my mom."

She walked the dog back onto the porch, where she could hear the sound of the television coming through the open screen door.

"Is it okay if I bring him in the house?"

"As long as he doesn't lift his leg on the furniture," came the hushed reply.

She leveled a look at the dog, who cocked his head at her. "Keep it together," she told him, and his stubby tail wagged again.

"I should get Charlie home and to bed," she said as she walked into the family room then stopped short. Sam sat on the couch, Charlie nestled into the crook of his arm, their attention riveted to the television. An IndyCar race was on the big set, and Sam was quietly explaining the details of the scene to Charlie.

"Lubock thinks he's got this one in the bag. He's in the blue-and-yellow car out front."

"Blue," Charlie said, his fist popping out of his mouth to point to the screen.

"That's right, but watch out for Eckhard in the red and white. See where he's coming around the outside?"

Charlie nodded drowsily then snuggled in deeper.

"I thought you didn't like kids," Julia said quietly, as Charlie's eyes drifted shut.

Sam glanced at the boy then tucked a blanket from the back of the couch around him. "I like kids. Everyone likes kids."

Julia scoffed. "Hardly. Most people like dogs. You don't."

"That's different."

She watched the pair for several seconds then added, "Charlie's father doesn't like kids."

Sam met her gaze. “His loss.”

“You’ve never even said hello to Charlie before this week.”

“He and I don’t run in the same circles,” he countered.

“You know what I mean.”

Sam picked up the remote and hit the mute button. He knew what she meant. Ever since he’d found Julia after her car crashed, he’d avoided both her and her son. That moment had terrified him more than it should someone in his position. He didn’t know whether it was the memory of losing his mother, or the strange way his body reacted to the woman sitting across from him. Or a combination of both. But when he’d lifted her out of that car and carried her to his cruiser, his instinct for danger had been on high alert.

Sam was used to saving people from mishaps. It was part of the job. But she’d looked at him as if she’d put all her faith in him. That had made it feel different. More real, and scary as hell. Charlie had been born that same day, and Sam had decided it was better for both of them if he stayed away. He had nothing to offer a single mom and her child. His heart had shut down a long time ago.

Holding Charlie in his arms, he felt something fierce and protective roar to life inside him. If he wasn’t careful, he could easily fall for this boy and his mother. He had to keep his distance but still play the part. His dad had spent most of the evening fawning over Julia and her son, leaving Sam blessedly alone.

He wanted to keep up the charade long enough for his father to leave town satisfied. When the eventual breakup came, Sam was sure he’d have a better chance of convincing Joe how heartbroken he was over the phone than in person.

“We should go over a few things before you leave,” he

said, trying to make his tone all business but soft enough that he didn't wake Charlie.

Julia nodded. "I can take him from you first."

Sam shook his head and adjusted the blanket. "He's fine. Thanks for bringing him. You saw how happy it made my dad."

"He's going to be devastated when this doesn't work out."

Sam shrugged. "He'll get over it. You've given him hope that I'm not a total lost cause in the commitment department. That should hold him over for a while."

Julia adjusted in her chair as the dog settled at her feet with a contented sigh. Sam had heard a lot about Vera Morgan's exceptional skills with animals. It appeared the gift was genetic.

"He mentioned your ex-girlfriend."

Sam flinched. If he didn't have Charlie sleeping against him, he would have gotten up to pace the room. "Leave it to dear old dad to knock the skeleton from my closet."

"We're engaged. He assumed I already knew."

"And you thought knowing my favorite color was going to be a big deal."

"We need to understand the details about each other if this is going to work. Otherwise, no one is going to believe we're legitimate."

"Why not?" he countered. "People run off to Vegas all the time. Maybe you fell so head over heels for me that you didn't care about the details."

"Highly unlikely. You're not that irresistible."

Her comeback made him smile, which he realized was her intention. It was strange that this woman he knew so little could read him so well. "I was engaged for six months. She cheated on me a month before the wedding."

"That's awful."

"I caught her with my brother."

Julia's jaw dropped. "Wow."

"That's an understatement."

"What happened? Do you still speak to your brother? Are they together? What kind of awful people would do that to someone they both loved?"

"The way Scott explained it, before I kicked him out of my house, was that she was bad news and he was saving me from making a mistake. The way Jenny spun it before she followed him out the door was that he'd seduced her." He expected to feel the familiar pain of betrayal but only emptiness washed over him. "They aren't together and weren't again as far as I know. Turns out he was right. I found out later it wasn't the first time she'd cheated. She'd also been with one of the guys on the squad. Made me look like a fool."

"She's the fool." Julia came to stand before him. She lifted Charlie from his arms and sat down, laying her son beside her on the soft leather. "And your brother?"

"Scott was in the army for several years. Now he works out of D.C. for the U.S. Marshals."

She squeezed his arm and the warmth of her hand relaxed him a little. "I'm not interested in his job. What about your relationship?"

"My dad had a health scare almost two years ago. I passed my brother in the hall at the hospital. That's the extent of it."

"Oh, Sam."

"We were never close. My dad didn't encourage family bonding."

"Still—"

"This isn't helping our arrangement." Sam took her hand in his. "How long have we been dating?"

"Four months," Julia answered automatically.

"Favorite color?"

"Blue."

"Where we going on a honeymoon?"

"A Disney cruise."

"You can't be serious."

"Because of Charlie."

He laughed. "Fine." Some of the tension eased out of his shoulders and he asked, "Big or small wedding?"

"Small, close friends and immediate family."

"Who are your close friends?"

Her eyes darted away and she took several beats to answer. "The girls from the salon, I guess. A few of them, anyway. My sister."

"What about your friends from high school?"

"I didn't really have friends. Followers was more like it, and most of them have outgrown me."

"Their loss," he said, using his earlier phrase, and was rewarded with a smile. "What about your ex-boyfriend? Do you still have feelings for him? Should I be jealous?"

"Of Jeff? No. We were over long before he left me."

An interesting way to phrase it. Sam couldn't help but ask, "Could I kick his butt?"

She smiled. "Absolutely."

"Good. When is your next court date?"

"Friday."

"Do you want me to come?"

She shook her head and Sam felt a surprising rush of disappointment. "I might be able to help."

"You already are."

"You can't believe the judge will award custody to Jeff and his family. Is he even going to be here?"

"I don't know. But I can't take any chances. Even if he gets joint custody, they could take Charlie from me for extended periods of time. I won't risk it. Jeff made it clear he didn't want to be a father, so I don't understand why he's letting this happen. He was never close to his family."

"Have you talked to him directly?"

"I left a message on his cell phone right after the letter came. I might have sounded hysterical. He hasn't returned my call."

"You're going to have to tell your family what's going on before it goes too much further."

She nodded. "I realized that tonight. If my mom finds out your dad knew before her… It's all too much. I'm finally starting to get my life on track, with the salon and Charlie. For the first time in as long as I can remember, my mother isn't looking at me with disappointment in her eyes. When she finds out…"

"Vera will want to help. This isn't your fault."

"It sure feels like it is." She sank back against the couch and scrubbed her hands across her face. Sam saw pain and fear etched in her features. It gnawed away at him until he couldn't stand it. Why was she so afraid of her mother's judgment? Why did she think so little of herself, to believe her son was at risk of being taken away? Maybe she'd made some mistakes in her past but Sam didn't know anyone who hadn't. She couldn't be punished forever.

He might not be willing to give his heart again, but he needed to give her some comfort. He wasn't great with words and knew that if he got sentimental, she'd only use her dry wit to turn it into a joke. Instead, he placed a soft kiss on the inside of her palm.

She tugged on her hand but he didn't let go. "You don't need to do that now," she whispered, her voice no more than a breath in the quiet. "There's no one watching."

One side of his mouth quirked. "It's a good thing, too, because what I want to do to you is best kept in private."

Her mouth formed a round *oh* and he lifted a finger to trace the soft flesh of her lips.

"Charlie."

"I know." He leaned closer. "You're safe tonight. Almost."

"We shouldn't…"

"I know," he repeated. "But I can't think of anything I want more."

"Me, too." She sat up and brought both of her hands to the sides of his face, cupping his jaw. "This isn't going to get complicated, right?"

"Other than planning a pretend wedding, a custody battle, my meddling father and a town filled with nosy neighbors? I think we can keep it fairly simple."

She smoothed her thumbs along his cheeks and her scent filled his head again. "I mean you and me. We're on the same page. It's all part of the show, the time spent together, pretending like we're in love. It ends when we both get what we want."

He agreed in theory, but at the moment all Sam wanted was her. He knew telling her that would make her more skittish than she already was. He didn't want this night to end quite yet, even if her sleeping son was going to keep the evening G-rated. So he answered, "That's the plan."

She nodded then licked her lips, and he suppressed a groan. "Then it won't matter if I do this…" She brought her mouth to his and they melted together. When her tongue mixed with his, he did groan. Or maybe Julia did. Her fingers wound through his hair and down his neck, pressing him closer, right where he wanted to be.

He deepened the kiss as his hands found their way underneath her blouse, his palms spread across the smooth skin on her back.

"Stop." Julia's breathing sounded ragged.

His hands stilled and he drew back enough to look into her big gray eyes, now hazy with desire.

A small smile played on the corners of her mouth. "I want to make sure we both stay in control. No getting carried away."

Like to his bedroom, Sam thought. All the wonderful, devilish, naked things he could do to her there ran through his brain. He wanted to know this woman—every inch of her—with a passion he hadn't thought himself capable of feeling.

He didn't answer, not sure his brain could manage a coherent sentence at the moment. They stared at each other and he wondered if Julia's heart was pounding as hard as his.

He heard Charlie snore softly and let his eyes drift closed for a few seconds. He counted to ten in his head, thought about the pile of work waiting in his office and tried like hell to rein in his desire and emotions.

He withdrew his hands, smoothed her shirt back down and forced a casual smile.

"My middle name is control, sweetheart."

She cocked her head. "That's a good point," she said and didn't sound at all as affected as Sam felt. "What *is* your middle name?"

He shook his head slightly. "Matthew."

"Mine's Christine," she told him, as if she had no memory of a minute earlier when she'd been kissing him as if her life depended on it. "I'm going to get Charlie home." She stood and picked up the sleeping boy. The Weimaraner jumped to attention and stayed close by her side.

Sam felt off balance at her switch in mood but didn't want to admit it. "I'll walk you to your car," he said, keeping the frustration out of his voice. This *was* a business arrangement, after all, passionate kissing aside. Maybe Julia had the right of it.

She nodded and grabbed the diaper bag, pushing it at Sam. "If you could carry that," she said, as if she didn't trust him with his hands free.

The night had cooled at least ten degrees and she shivered as she hurried down the front walk. "Do you want a jacket?" he asked, taking large strides to keep up with her.

"I'm fine."

While it might be true that Sam hadn't had any long-term relationships since moving to Brevia, and had stayed out of the dating pool totally for the past few months, his evenings never ended like this.

Usually he was the one who put the brakes on, sexually. More than once, he'd been invited back to a woman's house—or she'd asked to see his place—on the first date and gotten a clear signal that she'd been eager to take things to the next level. Sam was cautious and tried to not let an evening go there if he thought someone wanted more than he could give.

Never, until tonight, could he remember a woman literally running out of his house when he so badly wanted her to stay.

Julia opened the back door and placed Charlie in his car seat then gave the dog a little tug. The Weim jumped up without a sound, as if he knew enough not to wake the sleeping boy.

Turning, Julia held out her hand for the diaper bag.

"Are we good?" Sam asked.

"Yep," she said, again not meeting his gaze. "I'll talk to you in a few days."

A few days? They were engaged. He told himself it wouldn't look good to the town, but the truth was he couldn't wait a few days. Before he could respond, she'd scurried to the driver's side, climbing in with one last wave and "Thanks" thrown over her shoulder.

Sam was left standing alone at the curb, wondering what had gone so wrong so quickly. He headed back to the house, hoping a cold shower would help him make some sense of things.

Chapter Seven

Julia swiped under her eyes and focused her attention on her mug of lukewarm coffee, unable to make eye contact with her mother or sister.

Lainey paced the length of Vera's office in the All Creatures Great and Small animal shelter. By contrast, their mother sat stock-still behind her desk.

"That's the whole story," Julia finished. "The judge ordered us into mediation and that meeting is tomorrow morning. I don't think it will do any good. I know what I want and Jeff's parents know what they want. If we can't come to an agreement with the mediator, there will be a final hearing where the judge makes a ruling."

"Is Jeff going to be there?" Vera asked, her tone both soft and razor-sharp.

"I guess so, but it will be better if he isn't, if it looks like it's his parents who want this." Her breath hitched. "The latest document I got from their attorney asks for an every-other-year joint-custody arrangement. There's an opportunity for it to be amended if Charlie's well-being is in jeopardy with one of the parties."

"Every other year?" Lainey stopped pacing. "How can they think of taking him away from you for that long? You should have told us this as soon as you knew, Jules. Maybe we could have done something—"

"What, Lainey?" Julia snapped then sighed. "I'm sorry. I don't mean to take it out on you. But what could have been done? I hoped if I made it difficult for them, they might give up. The first letter said they wanted full custody and offered a hefty payment for the expenses I've already incurred in raising Charlie."

"They thought you'd sell them your son?" Lainey's voice was incredulous.

"That's one way of looking at it. The last Jeff knew, I'd gotten pregnant as a way to keep him. He could have told his parents I didn't really want to be a mother or wouldn't be able to handle it on my own."

"You're not on your own." Vera tapped one finger on the desk. "You have us. And Sam."

Conflicting emotions welled in Julia's chest again as she thought of Sam. He'd told her to talk to her mom and sister. She knew it was inevitable, so she'd called them both on the way home last night and asked them to meet her at the shelter before work. At the time, it had been a good way to distract herself from Sam and the way he made her feel.

He must have been baffled by her behavior after they'd kissed. Most women he knew could probably handle a simple kiss. Not Julia. Maybe it had been too long since she'd been in a man's arms. It had taken every ounce of her willpower not to beg him to take her to bed. His touch had rocked her to her core and she'd had to beat a quick retreat so she wouldn't do or say something she'd later regret.

When he'd proposed the pretend engagement, she'd had no idea how much her emotions would get in the way. She'd had no idea how it would affect her to see Sam cuddling Charlie against his broad chest. How much her body and heart would react to his arms around her. How quickly she'd come to depend on the comfort he gave her and how he made her feel strong by believing in her.

"I'm the one they're going after," she told her mom. "And Charlie." A sob escaped her lips and she clamped her hand over her mouth.

Lainey rushed to her side and Julia let herself be cradled in her sister's warm embrace. Silence descended over the trio. This was the time Julia would normally make a joke or sarcastic remark about her propensity to ruin her own life. But, right now, she was just struggling to not break down completely.

This was the reason she hadn't told her family. Their sympathy and the disappointment she felt from them brought back too many memories of the past and the feelings that went with it. Her LD and the shame that went with it had made her put up walls against everyone around her. She'd gotten used to getting by, keeping secrets, not letting on how bad things really were. It was a difficult pattern to break.

From the time she'd been younger, Julia had made an unintentional habit of disappointing the people she loved. She'd let other people's judgments guide the way she lived her life. The belief that she was lazy and stupid had stopped her from getting help so many times. It was easier not to open up to her family about her emotions. She was too afraid of being exposed as weak and lacking in their eyes.

Even when she'd shown up on her mother's doorstep, pregnant, broke and alone, she hadn't cried or offered long explanations or excuses. She just kept moving. Now she felt stuck in quicksand, as though nothing could save her.

Vera's palm slammed onto the desk. "We won't let this happen. Have you consulted Frank?"

Julia nodded. Frank Davis had been practicing law in Brevia for as long as she could remember and was a friend of her mother's. After Sam's suggestion that she see an attorney, she'd hired him to represent her. "He's helping with the case."

Vera nodded. "That's a good start. You need to talk to Jeff. To understand why he's doing this now when he had no previous interest in being a dad. Surely you'll be awarded sole custody. You're Charlie's mother and you do a wonderful job with him."

"I don't know, Mom. Jeff's family is arguing that they can give Charlie opportunities he'll never have with me."

"A child doesn't need anything more than a loving family. Let them set up a college trust if they're so concerned with opportunities."

"What do you want to see happen?" Lainey asked.

That question had kept Julia up many nights. "I'll support them having a relationship with Charlie. I'm sure as he gets older he'll have questions about his father's family. I want him to be surrounded by all the people who love him." She paused and took a breath. "I'm afraid he'll eventually choose them."

"He won't," Lainey said softly.

"You can't know that. But he needs to live with me now. Full-time. Swapping him back and forth is ludicrous."

"I'm going to the mediation," Vera announced.

Julia's stomach lurched. As much as she appreciated and needed her family's support, she was afraid it would only make her more nervous to have her mother with her.

"That's not a good idea. I appreciate the offer but I need to handle this on my own."

Lainey squeezed her shoulder and asked, "Has Jeff contacted you directly or tried to see Charlie?"

Julia shook her head. "No. Neither have his parents, other than when I got messages about discussing the custody arrangement."

"When did that start?" Vera came around the side of the desk.

"About a month ago. I ignored them until the certified letter arrived last week."

"Ignoring your problems doesn't make them go away."

Funny, it had always worked for Julia in the past. She'd taken the easy way out of every difficult situation that came her way before Charlie. And thanks to the complexity of her difficulties processing both words and numbers, problems seemed to plague her. From bad rental agreements to unfair terms on a car loan, her inability to manage the details of her life took its toll in a variety of ways. Still, nothing had prepared her for this.

A knock at the door interrupted them.

"Come in," Vera said.

A member of the shelter staff entered, leading in a gray dog. Or more accurately, the gray dog led her. Upon seeing Julia, the animal pulled at the leash, his stubby tail wagging. His lips drew back to expose his teeth.

"That's quite a greeting," Lainey said with a laugh.

"Sam thought it was a snarl when the dog first came at him." Julia bent to pet him. The dog wiggled and tried to put his front paws on her chest. She body blocked him. "Down."

"What's the report?" Vera asked the young woman.

"We've done his blood work and tested him for heartworm and parasites. Surprisingly, he got a clean bill of health."

"That's great." Julia felt relief wash over her. "Have you had any calls about a lost Weim?"

The young woman shook her head. "Not yet."

"We'll do a three-day hold before he moves onto the available-dog list." Vera dropped to her knees next to Julia. The dog lunged for her, teeth gleaming, but Vera held up a hand and gave a firm "No." The dog's rear end hit the carpet, although one corner of his mouth still curled.

Julia met her mother's gaze. "The smile's not good for him, is it?"

Vera shrugged. "It depends on the potential adopter, but a lot of people might think the same thing Sam did. We'll find a place for him. We always do."

Julia stroked the dog's silky ear. She'd planned on leaving the Weimaraner at the shelter this morning. "Can I foster him? Until the waiting period is over or someone shows interest. I'll work on basic training commands to help offset the shock of the smile."

Vera hesitated. "You've got a lot going on right now, honey. Weims aren't easy dogs. They can have separation anxiety and get destructive."

Frustration crept across Julia's neck and shoulders. "You know being in a foster home is better for a dog's well-being." She couldn't believe her mother would insinuate the dog would be better in the shelter than with her.

"Of course," Vera agreed, as if she realized she'd crossed some imaginary line. "If you're willing to, it would help him immensely."

"Have they named him yet?" Julia knew the shelter staff named each animal that came in to make their care more personal.

The young woman shook her head.

"Call him Casper," Julia said.

"The friendly gray ghost?" Lainey asked, referring to the breed's well-known nickname.

Julia nodded. "It fits him and will give people a sense of his personality."

"Perfect," her mother said then asked the young woman, "They've done a temperament test?"

She nodded. "He's a big sweetie." The walkie-talkie clipped to her belt hissed. "I'll finish the paperwork with Julia as the foster." When Vera nodded, the woman smiled and walked out of the office.

"It's settled." Julia was going to make sure this dog found the perfect home. She straightened. "Charlie will be thrilled."

She turned to her mother. "I need to get Charlie from Ethan and drop him to the sitter before heading to the salon."

"I'll take him today," her mother said, in the same no-argument tone she'd used earlier.

"Really? I'm sure your schedule is packed after your trip."

"I'd love to."

Julia gave her mother a quick hug. "Thank you." She turned to Lainey. "Both of you. It helps to know I'm not alone."

"You never have been," Vera told her.

"And never will be," Lainey added.

As she gave Charlie a bath later that night, Julia had to admit Sam had been right. Talking about the situation with Lainey and her mother had made her feel more hopeful. She might have flitted from job to job and through a number of cities during her twenties, but now she'd settled in Brevia. She was close to the point where she could make an offer to buy the salon, assuming this custody battle didn't wipe out her meager savings.

She wrapped Charlie in a fluffy towel, put on a fresh diaper and his pajamas, Casper at her side the whole time. She didn't mind the company. She'd taken him for a walk with Charlie in the stroller earlier, after the dog had spent the day with her in the salon.

A few of the clients had been shocked at his wide grin, but his affectionate nature had quickly won them over. It also made Julia feel more confident about his chances for adoption.

When the doorbell rang, Casper ran for it and began a steady bark. Carrying Charlie with her, she put a leash on the dog. A part of her hoped Sam was making another unexpected evening call.

Instead, Jeff Johnson stood on the other side of the door. Casper lunged for him but Julia held tight to the leash. She stumbled forward when the shock of seeing her ex-boyfriend combined with the dog's strength threw her off balance.

"Watch it," Jeff snapped as he righted her.

Casper smiled.

"What the…? Is that thing dangerous?" Jeff stepped back. "He looks rabid. You shouldn't have it near the baby. Are you crazy?"

"Casper, sit." Julia gave the command as she straightened. The dog sat, the skin around his mouth quivering. "Be careful, or I may give the attack command." She made her voice flip despite the flood of emotions roaring through her.

For a satisfying moment, Jeff looked as if he might make a run for it. Then his own lip curled. "Very funny."

"Good doggy." Charlie pointed at the canine.

"He talks," Jeff said, surprise clear.

"He does a lot of things," Julia answered, her eyes narrowed. "Not that you'd know or care since you beat a fast escape as soon as you found out I was pregnant."

Jeff flashed his most disarming smile, a little sheepish with his big chocolate eyes warm behind his square glasses. That exact smile had initially charmed her when he'd come in for a haircut at the salon where she'd worked in Columbus, Ohio.

For several months dating Jeff had been magical for her. He'd taken her to the theater and ballet, using his family's tickets. They'd gone to poetry readings and talks by famous authors on campus. Some of what she heard was difficult to process, and in a moment of vulnerability, she'd told Jeff about the extent of her learning disabilities. He'd been sympathetic and supportive, taking time over long evenings to read articles and stories to her, discussing them as if her opinion mattered. It was the first time in her life Julia felt valued for her intelligence, and she became committed to making their relationship work at any cost.

Soon she realized what a fool she'd been to think a well-respected professor would be truly interested in someone like her. It was clear that Jeff liked how his friends reacted when he'd shown up at dinner parties with a leggy blonde on his arm. He'd also gotten a lot of use out of the way she'd bent over backward cooking and cleaning to his exacting standards when she'd moved in with him. If she couldn't be on his level intellectually, she'd fulfill the other roles of a doting girlfriend. She'd wanted to believe that a baby would make him see how good their life together could be. She'd been dead wrong. Once she wasn't useful to him, he'd thrown her off like yesterday's news.

"Come on, Julia," he said softly, his grin holding steady. "Don't act like you aren't glad to see me." She'd been fooled by that smile once and wasn't going to make the same mistake again.

She flashed a smile of her own. "I don't see anyone throwing a ticker-tape parade. You can turn right around. I've got no use for you here."

"I'm here to see my son," Jeff said, as any trace of charm vanished.

Charlie met his biological father's gaze then buried his face in Julia's shoulder, suddenly shy.

"Why now, Jeff?" She rubbed a hand against Charlie's back when he began to fidget. "Why all of this now?"

He sighed. "The custody request, you mean."

Jeff's IQ was in the genius range, but sometimes he could be purposefully obtuse. "Of course the custody request. Do you know the hell you and your parents have put me through? We've barely scratched the surface."

"Invite me in, Jules," he said, coaxing, "and we can talk about it. I have an offer that may make this whole mess go away."

It had felt different when Sam stood at her door waiting to be invited through. Her stomach had danced with awareness and her only doubt had been worrying about her heart's exhilarated reaction to him. Still, Julia relented. If she had a chance to make this better, she couldn't refuse it.

Jeff stepped into her apartment but froze when Casper greeted him by sticking his snout into Jeff's crotch. "Get away, you stupid mutt." Jeff kicked out his foot, hitting Casper in the ribs. The dog growled.

"Casper, no." She pulled him back to her side with the leash then leveled a look at Jeff. "Don't kick my dog."

"It was going for my balls. What do you expect?"

"I wouldn't worry too much. As I remember, your mother keeps them on her mantel."

Jeff gave a humorless laugh. "Always one for the quick retort. I miss that about you."

"Good doggy. Charlie doggy." The boy wiggled in her arms and Julia put him on the floor. His chubby finger pulled the leash from her hand and he led the dog toward the kitchen. "Doggy nice." Casper followed willingly.

"You trust that beast with him?"

"More than I trust you." Julia folded her arms across her chest. "For the record, there's nothing I miss about you."

Jeff's eyes narrowed. "He's still my son. Whether you like it or not, I deserve to be a part of his life. There's no judge in the world who will deny me access."

"I never wanted to deny you access. I called you after he was born, emailed pictures and never heard one word back. You haven't answered my question. Why now?"

His gaze shifted to the floor. "Change of heart."

"You need a heart for it to change. You made it clear you never wanted to be a dad. What's the real story?" Before he could answer, Charlie led the dog back into the family room. He pulled a blanket off the couch and spread it on the floor. "Mama, doggy bed." She smiled as her son took a board book from the coffee table and sat on the blanket with Casper, making up words to an imaginary story.

Her gaze caught on Jeff, who yawned and looked around her apartment, obvious distaste written on his face for the kid-friendly decorating style. He didn't pay a bit of attention to his son. Since she'd opened the door, he'd barely looked at Charlie. It was the first time he'd laid eyes on his own flesh and blood. She realized he couldn't care less.

Unable to resist testing her theory, she said, "He's about to go to sleep. Do you want to read him a story? He loves books."

Jeff held up his palms as if she'd offered him a venomous snake. "No, thanks."

"I've got paperwork that says you want joint custody of my son. You act like you'd rather be dipped in boiling oil than have any interaction with him."

"I told you. I've got a proposition for you."

"What?"

"Marry me."

Julia stared at him, disbelief coursing through her. He couldn't have shocked her more if he'd offered her a million bucks. "Is that a joke? It's sick and wrong, but it must be a joke."

"I'm serious, Jules. You're right—I have no interest in being a father in any sense of the word. Ever. In fact—" he paused and ran his fingers through his hair "—I got a vasectomy."

"Excuse me?"

"After you, I was determined no woman would try to trap me again."

"It takes two. I'm sorry, Jeff, that I ever believed we could be a family. I know how wrong I was. But I don't understand why you've changed your mind now?"

"Are you kidding? I love my life. I've been on two research expeditions in the past year. I make my own schedule and can teach whatever classes I want. Why would I want to be tied down to a woman or a baby?"

"Then why are you suddenly proposing? Why the custody suit?"

Jeff had the grace to look embarrassed. "My parents found out about my surgery. It made them interested in our kid. You know I'm an only child. They expected me to marry and 'carry on the family line.'" He rolled his eyes. "Whatever. But my dad's company is a big funder of my grants. If he wants a grandchild, I need to give him one."

Julia's gaze strayed to Charlie, who was snuggled against Casper's back, sucking on his thumb. His eyes drifted closed. She felt a wave of nausea roll through her. "You need to *give* him one? And you think you're going to give him mine?"

Jeff shrugged. "Technically, he's *ours*. When my parents want something, they don't stop until they get it."

"How is anything you're saying good news for me? Why don't you get the hell out of my house and out of my son's life?"

"Not going to happen."

"When the judge finds out your plan…"

"No one is going to find out. I'm the father. You can't keep him from me."

"I want to keep him safe and protected."

"That's why you should marry me. Oh, I heard all about your engagement to the cop. He's not for you. I know you. You want someone who's going to make you look smart."

Julia sucked in a breath. "You have no idea what you're talking about."

"Does he know about your problem?"

When she didn't answer, Jeff smiled. "I thought so. I'm guessing you don't want him to. It hasn't come up in the court proceedings, either, but that can change. Here's my proposal. Marry me, move to Ohio. My parents' property is huge. They have a guesthouse where you can live with the boy. All of your expenses will be covered."

"Why would I agree to that, and what does it have to do with us being married?"

"A marriage will seem more legit to my parents' precious social circle. They'll get off my back with someone to shape and mold into their own image."

"Like they did you?"

"My parents are proud of me."

"I thought your father wanted you to give up the university and take over his business."

"Not going to happen."

"Instead, Charlie and I should spend our lives at their beck and call?"

"They'll keep fighting until they take him away from you. We all will."

Her temper about to blow, Julia yanked open the front door. "Get out, Jeff."

"On second thought, maybe I should read the kid a story. Get to know him before he comes to live with us."

"Get out!"

Jeff must have read something in her eyes that told him she would die before she let him touch her son tonight. He hesitated then turned for the door.

She slammed it behind him. The noise startled the dog and woke Charlie, who began to cry. She rushed over and cradled him in her arms.

"It's okay, sweetie. Mama's here." Tears streamed down her face as she hugged Charlie close. "No one's going to take you away from me. No one." She made the promise as much to herself as to him, wanting to believe the words were true.

Chapter Eight

Julia stepped into the afternoon light and put on her sunglasses, more to hide the unshed tears welling in her eyes than for sun protection.

Frank Davis, her attorney, took her elbow to guide her down the steps of the county courthouse. They'd spent the past two hours in a heated session with Jeff, his parents and their lawyer. She couldn't believe how much information they'd dug up, from the details of her finances, including the business loan that had yet to be approved, to her credit history. Thanks to a loser boyfriend who'd stolen her bank-account information, her credit was spotty, at best.

They knew all of the dead-end jobs she'd had over the years, including those she'd been fired from or quit without notice, and had a detailed record of her habit of moving from city to city for short periods of time.

They'd brought in statements from one of her ex-boyfriends and a former employer stating she was flighty and irresponsible. Her old boss even said that she'd threatened to set fire to her hair salon. No one mentioned the woman had skimmed Julia's paycheck without her knowledge for over nine months after she'd discovered Julia's learning disabilities. Torching the place had been an idle threat, of course, but it hadn't sounded that way today.

"They made me seem crazy," she muttered.

Frank clucked softly. "It's all right, darlin'. A lot of mamas in the South are a bit touched. No one around here's gonna hold that against you." He checked his watch. "I got a tee time with some of the boys at one. Give me a call tomorrow and we'll plan our next move." He leaned in and planted a fatherly kiss on her cheek, then moved toward his vintage Cadillac parked at the curb.

Frank had known her since she'd been in diapers. He'd been one of her father's fraternity brothers in college. Not for the first time, she questioned the wisdom of hiring him to represent her. It was no secret Frank was close to retirement, and from what Julia could tell, he spent more time on the golf course and fishing with his friends than in his office or working on cases.

Lexi Preston might look like a pussycat, but she was an absolute shark. From her guilty expression every time they made eye contact, Julia knew Lexi was the one who'd researched her so thoroughly. Julia would have admired her skills if they hadn't been directed at her.

She glanced toward the courthouse entrance. Jeff and his parents could come out at any minute and she didn't want them to see her alone and on the verge of a breakdown. She wished now that she'd let her mother or Lainey come with her today.

She turned to make her way to her car and came face-to-face with Sam.

"Hey," he said softly and drew the sunglasses off her

nose, his eyes studying hers as if he could read what she was thinking. "How did things go today?"

"I told you not to come," she said on a shaky breath.

"I don't take direction well." He folded her glasses and pulled her into a tight embrace. "It's okay, honey. Whatever happened, we can make it better."

She tried to pull away but he didn't let her go. After a moment, she sagged against him, burying her face in the fabric of his uniform shirt.

As his palm drew circles on her back, her tears flowed freely. She gulped in ragged breaths. "So awful," she said around sobs. "They made me seem so awful."

"I don't believe that," he said against her ear. "Anyone who knows you knows you're a fantastic mother."

"What if they take him from me?"

"We're not going to let that happen. Not a snowball's chance."

Julia wiped her eyes. "They're going to come out any minute. Jeff can't see me like this."

"My truck's right here." Sam looped one arm around her shoulders, leading her away from the courthouse steps. He opened the passenger door of his truck then came around and climbed in himself. He started the engine but didn't make a move to drive off.

Julia kept her face covered with her hands and worked to control her breathing.

"Is that him?" Sam asked after a minute.

Julia peeked through her fingers as Jeff, his parents and the attorney walked out of the courthouse. Shading his eyes with one hand, Jeff scanned the area.

"He's looking for me so he can gloat." Julia sank down lower in the seat. "Jerk," she mumbled.

The group came down the steps.

"They're heading right for us."

"Sit up," Sam ordered, and she immediately straightened. "Smile and lean over to kiss me when they come by."

The urge to duck was huge, but Julia made her mouth turn up at the ends. "Here goes," she whispered as Jeff led the group closer, his father clapping him hard on the back. She waited until he noticed her through the windshield then leaned over and cupped Sam's jaw between her hands. She gave him a gentle kiss and pressed her forehead against his.

"That a girl," he told her. "Don't give him the satisfaction of seeing you upset."

"I can do this," she said, and Sam kissed her again.

"They've passed."

Julia stayed pressed against him for another moment before moving away. She leaned against the seat back in order to see out the side-view mirror. Jeff and his parents headed away, but Lexi trailed behind the group, looking over her shoulder every few steps.

"This isn't going to work."

"Yes, it is."

She shook her head. "I told you before, I made a lot of stupid decisions in my life. It's like they've uncovered every single one of them to use against me."

"Did you kill someone?"

Her head whipped toward him. "Of course not."

"Armed robbery?"

"No."

"Do you know how many people I meet in the course of my job who do bad things every day? Their kids are rarely taken away."

"Maybe they should be," she suggested, too unsettled to be comforted. "Maybe if they had people with buckets of money and tons of power going after them, they'd lose their babies."

He wrapped his fingers around hers. "You aren't going to lose Charlie. Stop thinking like that."

"You don't know, Sam. You weren't in that room."

"A mistake I don't intend to repeat. I should have been there with you. For you."

The tenderness in his voice touched a place deep within her: an intimate, open well of emotion she'd locked the lid to many years ago. She wanted to believe in him, to trust that he could protect her the way she'd never been willing to protect herself or even believed she deserved. The part of her who'd been hurt too many times in the past wanted to run.

She excelled at running away. She'd practically perfected it as an art.

That was what she'd been thinking in the courthouse. People disappeared all the time with no trace. She'd wanted to slip out of that room, gather up Charlie and whatever would fit in her trunk and drive away from the threat looming over her. She could cut hair anywhere. Why not start over in a place where no one knew her or her insecurities or all the ways she didn't measure up? She had friends around the country who'd help her if she asked.

The weight of trying to make a new life in a place that was as familiar to her as a worn blanket seemed too heavy. Of course trouble had followed her to Brevia. This was where it had started in the first place.

Sam's faith had made her feel as though things could work out, the same way Charlie's birth had renewed her hope in herself and her desire to really try.

What was the use? This morning was a cold, harsh dose of reality and she didn't like it.

"Stop it," he said quietly. "Whatever's going through your mind right now, put it out. It's not going to do you or Charlie any good for you to give up."

Because she couldn't help it, she met his gaze again. "I'm scared, Sam." A miserable groan escaped her lips. "I'm terrified they're going to take my baby and I won't be able to stop them."

"We're going to stop them." He took her hand. "What did Frank say?"

"That all Southern women were crazy, so it wouldn't be an issue, and he needed to make his tee time and we'd talk tomorrow."

"Tell me what happened in there."

"I can't." She bit her lip again and tasted blood on her tongue. "I put my mistakes behind me. Or I thought I did. Their attorney knew things about my past I hadn't even told Jeff. They went after my character and I had nothing to offer in my defense. Nothing as bad as me killing someone, although the urge to wipe the smug smile off of Maria Johnson's face was almost overwhelming. They made me seem unstable and irresponsible. Two things I can't afford if I'm going to keep sole custody of Charlie."

"Then we'll come up with something."

"This isn't your problem, Sam."

"Hell, yes, it's my problem. You're my fiancée."

The lunacy of that statement actually made her laugh. "Your fake fiancée. Not the same thing."

"For the purposes of your custody case it is. You're not alone, Julia. We both get something out of this arrangement. My dad has talked about heading back home before the wedding. That's huge for me. Dinner was a big success. It's my turn to repay you."

Sam knew there was more to his interest in her case than wanting to repay her. Yes, his dad had backed off, but it was more than that. Sam cared about Julia and Charlie, about keeping them safe. No one should be able to make her feel this bad about herself. He also knew it was dangerous territory for him. He'd let his heart lead him before, with disastrous results.

His father might be the king of emotional diarrhea these days, but Sam remembered clearly the months after his mother's death. He'd fixed lunches for his little brother, made sure they both had baths at night and taken money out of his dad's wallet to buy groceries on his way home from school. He'd walked a mile out of his way once a week so no one at the local grocery would recognize him and be concerned. When he wasn't at work, his father had sat in the darkened living room, paging through photo albums, a glass of amber-colored liquid in his hand.

That was what loving someone too much could do to a man. Sam had learned early on he wasn't going to make that mistake. When he'd caught his brother, Scott, with his ex-fiancée, he'd been angry and embarrassed, but mainly numb.

When he'd broken off the engagement, Jenny had told him the entire situation was his fault. He'd been too cold and distant. She wanted to be with a man who could feel passion. She'd thought seeing her with someone else would awaken Sam's passion. Talk about crazy, and she wasn't even Southern.

He'd known he didn't have any more to give her or any woman. Even though his pattern of dating hadn't been deliberate, the look a woman sometimes got in her eye after a couple of dates scared him. The look said "I want something more." She wanted to talk about her feelings. Sam felt sick thinking about it.

As far as he was concerned, a pretend engagement suited him fine. He cared about Julia and he wanted to help her, but their arrangement was clear. He didn't have to give more of himself than he was able to, and she wasn't going to expect anything else.

"Jeff asked me to marry him," she said, breaking his reverie.

"During the mediation?" he asked, sure he must have heard her wrong.

She shook her head. "Last night. He came to my apartment."

Sam felt his blood pressure skyrocket. "You let him in? What were you thinking?" Especially since Sam had practically had to hold himself back from making the short drive to her apartment. He'd had a long day at work, and as he was pulling into his driveway, he'd realized how much he didn't want to be alone in his quiet house. He'd resisted the urge, telling himself that he shouldn't get too attached to Julia or her son. They had boundaries and he was a stickler for the rules. Now to find out that her creep of an ex-boyfriend had been there?

"He came crawling back." Sam kept his tone casual. Inside, his emotions were in turmoil. This was the guy she'd wanted to marry so badly. What if she still carried a torch for him? He'd obviously been an idiot to let her go once. If he came back now, trying to rekindle a romance and wanting to be a real family, would Julia consider taking him back? That thought hit Sam straight in the gut. "What did you say?"

She studied him for a moment. "He didn't quite come crawling. More like trumpeting his own horn. He told me the reason they're coming after Charlie is because his parents want an heir to the family business."

"They've got a son. Let him take over."

"Not his deal, and Jeff isn't going to have other children. He's made sure of that. Although it's crazy to think they could start grooming a mere toddler. No wonder Jeff has so many issues. If only I'd been smart enough to see it when we were together. You know what the strange part of this is? No one in Jeff's family has tried to get to know Charlie. It's like they want him on paper but they don't care about having a grandson. I want him to know their family if they have a real interest in him. But I saw how Jeff suffered from being a pawn in his parents' power games. I can't let the same thing happen to Charlie."

He held her hand, his brilliant blue eyes warm with emotion. "Your son needs you. He needs you to fight for him."

She nodded and wiped at her nose.

"What you need is a plan of defense. You flaked on some jobs. It happens."

"There's a reason," she mumbled, almost reluctantly.

"A reason that will explain it away?"

She shrugged and shook free from his hand, adjusting the vents to the air-conditioning as a way to keep her fingers occupied. "I have severe learning disabilities."

When he didn't respond she continued, "I've been keeping it a secret since I was a kid. It's a neurobiological disorder, both visual and auditory. Only my family and a few teachers knew, and I kept it from them for as long as I could. Everyone else assumed I was lazy or didn't care."

"Why would you hide that?"

"You have no idea what it's like, how much shame and embarrassment is involved. To people who've never dealt with it, it seems cut-and-dried. It's not." Her hands clenched into fists as she struggled with her next words. "I'm a good mimic and my bad attitude served me well as a way to keep everyone from digging too much. I got by okay, but I can barely read. Numbers on a page are a puzzle."

"All those books on your shelf..."

"I'm nothing if not determined. I'll get through them someday. Right now, I'm working with a literacy specialist. They have a lot of methods that weren't available when

I was in school. But it never gets easier. For years, I tried so hard in school but people thought I was a total slacker. Ditzy blonde cheerleader with no brain. A lot of the time that's how it felt. Once I was out on my own, I hid it as best I could. People can take advantage of me pretty easily when it comes to contracts or finances. And that's what happened. A number of times. It always seemed easier to just move on rather than to fight them."

"Every time someone got wind of it, you left."

She nodded. "It was cowardly but I don't want to be treated like I'm stupid. Although, looking back, I acted pretty dumb most of the time. Especially when it came to boyfriends. I trusted Jeff. He never let me forget it."

"That you had a learning disability?"

"That I'm just a pretty face. The blond hair and long legs. When I told him I was pregnant, he told me that once my looks faded I wouldn't have anything left to offer."

"He's a real piece of work." Sam couldn't believe how angry he was. At her idiot ex-boyfriend and all the others who took advantage of her. But also with Julia. Watching her, Sam could tell she believed the garbage people had fed her over the years. He threw the truck into gear, not wanting to lose his temper. "Where's your car?"

"Around the corner." She pointed then shifted in her seat. "Thanks for coming today, Sam. I was a mess after the mediation. You helped."

"I could have helped more if you'd let me be in there with you." He pulled out from the curb and turned onto the next street. Her car was parked a few spaces down.

"Maybe next time," she said quietly. She reached for the door handle but he took her arm.

"You have a lot more to offer than looks. Any guy who can't see that is either blind or an enormous jackass." He kept his gaze out the front window, afraid of giving away too much if he looked at her.

"Thanks."

He heard the catch in her voice and released her. After she'd shut the door, he rolled down the window. "The Mardi Gras Carnival is tonight. I'll pick you and Charlie up at five."

"I'm beat. I wasn't planning on going."

"I'll pick you up at five. You need to take your mind off this, and it's a good place for us to be seen together."

Her chest rose and fell. "Fine. We'll be ready."

After she'd gotten into her car, Sam pulled away. Although the air was hot for mid-March, he shut the windows. Julia's scent hovered in the truck's cab. Sam wanted to keep it with him as long as he could.

He'd meant what he said about taking her mind off today. As police chief, he was obligated to make an appearance at town events, but he looked forward to tonight knowing he'd have Julia and Charlie with him.

Chapter Nine

Julia dabbed on a bit of lip gloss just as the doorbell rang. She picked up Charlie, who was petting Casper through the wire crate.

"Let's go."

"'Bye, doggy."

Casper whined softly.

"We'll be back soon," Julia told him. The doorbell rang again. "Coming," she called.

She grabbed the diaper bag off the table and opened the front door, adjusting her short, flowing minidress as she did.

"We're ready."

"Sammy," Charlie said, bouncing up and down in her arms.

"Hey, bud." Sam held out his hands and Charlie dived forward.

Julia worried for a moment about Charlie bonding so

quickly with Sam. In a way it worked to their advantage, at least as their pretend engagement went. But she had concerns about Charlie's clear affection for Sam. She didn't want her son to be hurt once their time together ended.

"You don't have to take him."

"My pleasure." Sam looked her over from head to toe then whistled softly. "You look amazing."

Julia felt a blush creep up her cheeks. "You, too."

It was true. Tonight he wore a light polo shirt and dark blue jeans. His hair was still longer and her fingers pulsed as she thought about running them through the ends. He hadn't shaved, and the dusting of short whiskers along his jaw made him look wilder than he normally did as police chief.

It excited her more than she cared to admit. She hadn't been on a real date in over two years. This wasn't real, she reminded herself. This was showing off for the town, convincing people their relationship was genuine.

Not that being in this relationship had helped her earlier. She'd barely said two words in her own defense as the Johnsons' attorney had put forward more and more information about her deficiencies as a person and how they might be detrimental to raising her son.

The mediator, an older woman who was all business, hadn't said much, nodding as she took in everything and occasionally looking over her glasses to stare at Julia.

Sam was right. She needed to get her mind off the custody case. So what if this night wasn't a real date and Sam wasn't her real boyfriend? It wouldn't stop her from enjoying herself.

Because of Charlie's car seat, she drove. Once they were close to the high school, she could see the line of cars. Half the town was at the carnival. She knew Lainey and Ethan would be there along with her mother.

"Is your dad coming tonight?" she asked, a thought suddenly blasting across her mind.

Sam nodded. "I told him we'll meet him."

"My mom is, too."

Sam made a choking sound. "Okay, good. They can get to know each other. It'll be great."

"That's one word for it."

"Does your mom believe the engagement? I haven't seen her since she walked in on us."

"I think so." Julia slowed to turn into the lower parking lot. "It's not the first time she's seen me be impulsive."

Sam shook his head as she turned off the ignition. "You never give yourself a break."

"Why do I deserve one?" She paused then said, "It's fine. I'm repairing my reputation with my family. It's a long progress, but I'm getting there. What makes you ask about my mom?"

"I saw Ethan downtown yesterday and he gave me the third degree about my intentions toward you."

"Ethan?"

"His big-brother routine was going strong. Told me how special you are and that if I hurt you or Charlie I'd have him to answer to."

"I don't know why he'd care. He went through hell because of me, although it's ancient history now."

"There you go again with the self-flagellation. We're going to need to work on that."

"Whatever you say." She got out of the car and picked up Charlie from his car seat. As she turned, she took in her old high school. It looked the same as it had almost fifteen years ago.

She filled her lungs with the cool night air. This was her favorite time of year in the North Carolina mountains. It smelled fresh and clean, the scent of spring reminding her of new beginnings. Coming off of the cold, wet winter, the change of seasons gave her hope.

Just like Sam.

Julia knew hope was dangerous. She was a sucker for believing in things that would never come to pass. She'd been like that in high school, too—wanting to believe she'd be able to keep up. Or, at least, admit how deeply her problem ran.

For some reason, that never seemed an option. Sam could say what he wanted about her learning disabilities being beyond her control. She knew it was true. But by high school, when elementary-age kids read more clearly than she could, it felt like stupidity.

None of her teachers had understood what was going on in her head. She'd never truly opened up to anyone about how bad it was. It had been easier to act as though she didn't care, to limp through school with a lot of blustering attitude and paying smarter kids to write her papers.

Charlie tapped her on the cheek. "Hi, Mama."

She shook off the memories. Sam stood next to her, watching with his too-knowing eyes.

"I'm guessing you haven't been back here for a while?"

"Not since graduation." She adjusted Charlie and headed for the gymnasium entrance. "Remind me again why we're here."

Sam put his hand on the small of her back, the gentle touch oddly comforting. "The annual Kiwanis carnival not only celebrates Fat Tuesday but raises a lot of money each year for local kids. It's a great event for the town."

"Spoken like a true pillar of the community." She gave an involuntary shiver. "Which I'm not and never will be."

"You never know. Either way, I promise you'll have fun. Greasy food, games, dancing."

Since she'd been back, she hadn't attended any town

events. It was one thing to reconnect with people she'd known within the relative safety of the salon. No one was going to rehash old resentments while she wielded scissors. Here she was out of her element and not confident about the reception she'd get from the girls she once knew. Especially since she'd taken Brevia's most eligible bachelor off the market.

A memory niggled at the back of her mind. "Didn't you do a kissing booth last year or something like that?"

Sam's confident stride faltered. "They auctioned off dates with a couple local guys."

She flashed him a smile. "How much did you go for, Chief?"

In the fading light, she saw a distinct trail of red creep up his neck. "I don't remember."

"Liar." She stood in one spot until he turned to look at her. "Tell me."

"A thousand," he mumbled.

"Dollars?" She gasped. "Who in the world paid that much money for you?" When he leveled a look at her, she added, "Not that I don't think you're worth it. But not a lot of people around here have that kind of cash."

"It was for a good cause" was his only answer.

Another thought struck. "Unless…it was Ida Garvey!"

He turned and she trotted to catch up with him, Charlie bouncing on her hip. "Let me take him." Sam slid his arms around Charlie and scooped him up.

"It was Ida, wasn't it? She's the only one around here rich enough to pay that amount."

He gave a reluctant nod. "I got the most money."

"What kind of date did you take her on?"

"Would you believe I escorted her to her fiftieth high-school reunion over in Asheville? She had me wait on her hand and foot. Kept calling me her 'boy toy' in front of her old friends." He shook his head. "I swear my butt had bruises from being pinched so often."

Julia laughed harder than she had in ages. "You really are a hero, you know?"

"It's not funny."

"Yes, it is." She looked at him and saw humor shining in his eyes, as well. Then she noticed they were at the gym entrance, light spilling out into the darkening night. She studied Sam for another moment, wondering if he'd told her that story to ease her nerves.

He really was a good guy, she thought. He should be with someone like him—a woman who was smart and sweet.

Someone nothing like her.

He smoothed the skin between her eyebrows. "Stop frowning," he said gently. "We're going to have fun."

He dropped his hand, intertwined his fingers with hers and led her into the gymnasium. He greeted the two women working the ticket counter, neither of whom Julia recognized. Sam made introductions, and both women gave her a genuine smile and shook her hand, offering congratulations on their engagement. She flashed her ring but noticed Sam stiffen when one of the ladies complimented him on it.

Charlie became suddenly shy and buried his face in the crook of Sam's neck, something Julia would have loved to do, as well.

"Come on, buddy," Sam coaxed. "Let's find some cotton candy."

"I don't think so," Julia said. "He hasn't had dinner yet."

Charlie gave Sam a wide grin. "Can-ee."

"We'll get a hot dog first," Sam promised her and moved into the crowd.

"Kids can always count on their dad for a good time," one of the women said with a laugh.

"While Mom cleans up the sick stomach," the other added.

"He's not..." Julia began, wanting to explain that Sam wasn't her son's father. Then she realized they already knew that, although Sam was certainly acting like the doting dad.

"He's quite a catch." The blonder of the two women winked at her.

Julia's stomach flipped because she knew how right the woman's statement was. "I'd better stick with them," she said and hurried after the two, emotions already at war in her mind and heart.

"Julia!" Lainey's voice carried over the crowd, and a moment later, she was surrounded by her sister, Ethan and their mother. Lainey gave her a long hug. "Sam said today was rough. Are you feeling any better?"

"I knew I should have come with you." Vera shook her head. "I'd like to get ahold of that family and talk some sense into them."

"When did you see Sam?" The thought of Sam giving information about her to her family made her more than a little uncomfortable.

"I ran into him downtown," Lainey said. "What's the big deal?"

"He shouldn't have said anything."

"He's going to be your husband," Vera corrected. "He has a right to worry."

"We all do," Lainey echoed. "Jules, you've got to let us help you. You're not alone."

"Where's the little man?" Ethan asked, his internal radar about conflict between the three Morgan women practically glowing bright red through his T-shirt.

"Right here," Sam answered, balancing a huge cotton

candy and a paper plate with hot-dog chunks and small pieces of watermelon on it.

Charlie reached for a piece of fruit and babbled a few nonsense words.

"You cut up the hot dog," Julia said, stunned.

Sam's forehead wrinkled. "I thought you were supposed to cut up round food when kids are little."

"You are." Julia felt ridiculous that something so minor had such an effect on her emotions. "I didn't realize you'd know it."

"Don't be silly." Vera reached for Charlie and snuggled him against her. "He's spent enough time around you and Charlie to realize that."

Julia saw Lainey studying her, a thoughtful expression on her face. "That's right. Isn't it, Jules?"

Julia nodded and stepped next to Sam, leaning up to kiss him on the cheek. "Of course. Thanks, hon."

Lainey's features relaxed and Julia blew out a quiet breath of relief.

"There's my favorite son and future daughter-in-law." So much for her short-lived relief. Julia heard Sam groan.

She turned and was enveloped in one of Joe Callahan's bear hugs. He moved from her to Sam. "Look at you, Sammy. Surrounded by friends with the woman you love at your side." His meaty hands clasped either side of Sam's jaw. "I'm so proud of you, son. You're not a loner anymore. I thought my mistakes had cost you a chance at a real life. But you're making it happen."

"Dad, enough." Sam pulled Joe's hands away. "Not the time or the place."

"There's always time to say 'I love you.'"

Sam met Julia's gaze over his father's shoulders. His eyes screamed "help me," and as fascinating as everyone seemed to find the father-son interaction, she intervened.

"Joe, I'd like you to meet my family."

He turned, his smile a mile wide.

"This is my sister, Lainey, and her husband, Ethan Daniels."

Joe pumped their hands enthusiastically. "Pleasure to meet you both. I'm Joe Callahan."

"Are you in town for long, Mr. Callahan?" Lainey asked.

"As long as it takes," Joe said with a wink at Sam.

A muscle in Sam's jaw ticked and his eyes drifted shut as he muttered to himself. They flew open a moment later when Ethan added, "You, Sammy and I should do some fishing once the weather warms up."

"Don't call me Sammy."

"I'd love to."

Vera cleared her throat.

"Sorry. This is my mother, Vera Morgan. And you've met Charlie."

Joe's eyes widened as he looked at Vera. "Well, I certainly see where you two girls get your beauty. Ms. Morgan, you are a sight to behold."

Vera held out her hand like the Southern belle she'd once been. Joe bent over her fingers and kissed them lightly. "Why, Mr. Callahan," she said, her accent getting thicker with every syllable. "You are a silver-tongued devil, I believe."

"Shoot me now," Sam muttered.

Julia's eyes rolled. She was used to this routine with her mother. Vera had been a devoted wife to her late husband, but since his death, she'd reinvented herself not only as an animal-rescue expert but as a woman with a long list of admirers. Unlike Julia, her mother always made sure the men with whom she was acquainted treated her like a lady, fawning around her until Vera moved on to the next one in line.

"Here she goes," Lainey whispered, as Vera tucked her chin and fluttered her eyelashes. Charlie watched the two for a moment then reached for Sam.

"Can-ee," the boy demanded, and Joe took the cotton candy from Sam.

"Come here, Charlie," Joe said and lifted him from Vera's arms. At this rate, Charlie would be held by more people than the Stanley Cup.

"Why don't I take him," Julia suggested.

"Joe and I will take him to the carnival games," Vera said.

"That's right," Joe told them with a wink. "You young folks can head to the dance floor or grab a drink."

Before she could argue, Joe and Vera disappeared into the sea of people, Charlie waving over Joe's shoulder.

"I'm up for a beer." Ethan looked at Sam. "How about you, Sammy boy?"

"Don't go there," Sam warned.

"Stop—you're going to make me cry." Ethan laughed until Lainey socked him in the gut. "Hey," he said on a cough.

"I thought Sam's dad was sweet." Lainey grinned at Sam. "He obviously loves you." Her gaze switched to Julia. "You and Charlie, too. Mom's going to eat him up with a spoon."

"A terrifying thought." Julia'd known this night was a bad idea.

"Come on," Lainey said to all three of them. "Let's get something to eat. They had a pasta booth in the corner."

Ethan wrapped one long arm around Lainey and kissed the top of her head. "Yeah, like a double date."

Julia couldn't help it—she burst out laughing. "This is going to be great. We'll be besties." Who would have thought that she'd be double-dating with her first boyfriend and her sister? It was too crazy to imagine.

She looked at Sam, expecting him to be laughing right along with her. Instead, his brows were drawn low over his vivid blue eyes.

"Fine by me." He took her hand to follow Lainey and Ethan toward the back of the gym.

"What's wrong?" she whispered, pulling him to slow down so they were out of hearing range. "Is it my mom and Joe? She's harmless, I promise. Her former admirers still adore her. Whatever happens, she won't hurt your dad."

Sam's arm was solid as a rock as his muscles tensed. "Does it seem strange to be so chummy with your ex-boyfriend?"

Julia thought about Jeff, then realized that was not who Sam meant. "Ethan's married to my sister. We've been over more than a decade. He's so much like my brother, I barely remember he's seen me naked."

Sam stopped on a dime, causing her to bump into the length of him. "Is that a joke?"

She wrinkled her nose. "I thought it was funny."

"It's not."

"Come on, Sam. You see how he looks at Lainey. He never once looked at me in that way. He's different with her, and I couldn't be happier. For both of them. It's old news, even around Brevia. That's an accomplishment, given how gossip takes on a life of its own in this town." She flashed him a sassy grin. "Chief Callahan, is it possible you're jealous?"

"I don't want to look like a fool. I've been down the road of public humiliation and the scenery sucks. Why would I be jealous? You said yourself Ethan's like your brother."

Julia studied him then placed a soft kiss on his mouth.

"I'd never do something to make you look like a fool. Scout's honor."

"I can't imagine you as a Girl Scout." Sam forced his lips to curve into a smile, wondering at his odd reaction. He wasn't the jealous type, and he knew how happy Ethan and Lainey were together. "Let's find them." He took Julia's hand again.

A number of people waved or stopped to say hello as they made their way through the crowd. At first, Julia tensed at every new greeting. Eventually he felt her relax, but she never loosened her death grip on his hand. He wanted to protect her, he realized, and also to show her she could belong to this community again. The people of Brevia had welcomed him, and if Julia gave them a chance, he was sure they'd accept her.

They caught up with Ethan and Lainey and grabbed a table near the makeshift dance floor. The sisters bantered back and forth, making Sam wish for a better relationship with his own brother.

Even before Scott had cheated with Sam's fiancée, they hadn't been close. Sam had been the responsible brother, stoic and toeing the line, while Scott had been wild, always getting into trouble and constantly resenting his older brother's interference in his life.

"How are things around town these days?" Ethan asked as he set a second beer on the table next to Sam.

"Quiet for a change." Sam took another bite of pasta then swallowed hard as Julia tilted back her head to laugh at something Lainey said. The column of her neck was smooth and long. He ached to trail a line of kisses across her skin.

He pushed away the beer, realizing he was going to need his wits about him to remain in control tonight.

"Were you involved in the drug bust over in Tellet County a few nights back?"

Julia stopped midsentence as her eyes snapped to his. "What drug bust? Sounds dangerous. Why didn't I hear about a drug bust?"

Sam threw Ethan what he hoped was a *shut your mouth* look.

"Sorry, man," Ethan said quickly. "Hey, Lainey, let's hit the dance floor."

Lainey popped out of her chair. "Love to."

"Cowards," Julia muttered as she watched them go. She turned her angry gaze back to Sam. "You were saying?"

"A meth lab outside the county lines," he told her. It had been a long time since anyone had cared about what he was doing and whether it was dangerous or not. "It's been kept quiet so far because the sheriff thinks it's part of a bigger tristate operation. We want to see if we can flush out a couple of the bigger fish."

She tapped one finger on the table. "I don't like you being involved in something like that."

"It's my job, Julia."

"I need to know about these things. I bet Abby Brighton knew where you were during the drug bust."

"She's my secretary. Of course she knew."

"We're engaged."

"Is that so?"

To his great amusement, she squirmed in her chair. "As far as everyone around here thinks. I need to be kept informed."

"Why?"

"To know whether I should worry."

"One more reason I wouldn't be a good bet in a real relationship. Ask my ex. I don't like to report in. I don't like anyone worried about me." He blew out a frustrated breath. "My job is dangerous almost every day. I deal with it, but I don't expect you or anyone else to."

"No one's allowed to care about you?" Her eyes flashed, temper lighting them.

"I don't need anyone to care."

"The Lone Ranger rides again." Julia pushed away from the table. He grabbed her wrist so she couldn't escape.

"Why are you mad? This doesn't have anything to do with you. We have a business arrangement. That's what we both wanted. It's not going to help either of us to be emotionally involved with the other one's life."

"Some of us care, whether we want to or not."

Her eyes shone and his heart leaped in his chest. He pulled her tight against him, aware they were gathering stares from people standing nearby. "Thank you for caring. I'm not used to it, but it means a lot." He pressed his forehead to hers. "I'm sorry I'm bad at this. Even for pretend."

"You're not *so* bad," she whispered.

"Do you want to dance?"

"Do you?"

He grinned at her. "Hell, no. But I can make it work."

"Give me a minute. I need to catch up with my mom and Joe, make sure Charlie's okay."

He studied her. "If I didn't know better, I'd say you're avoiding me right now."

She shook her head. "I want to find Charlie."

"They headed back toward the game booths. I'm going to say hi to the mayor and I'll meet you over there."

The gym was full, and without Sam at her side, Julia got a little panicked by the crowd.

She moved toward the far end of the gymnasium where the carnival booths were set up, then veered off quickly when she saw two women from her high-school class standing together near one of the attractions. One was

Annabeth Sullivan, whom Julia felt friendlier toward after their conversation at the salon. The other was Lucy Peterson, their graduating class's valedictorian. Julia had always been uncomfortable around her. She'd made it clear during high school that Lucy was persona non grata and knew the slightly chubby teen had suffered because of it.

Lucy had gotten her revenge, though. Because of her work in the school office and her access to the files, she'd found out about Julia's learning disabilities. She hadn't told anyone outright, but had spread the rumor that Julia had only graduated because she'd slept with one of her teachers and he'd fixed her grade.

She'd told Julia that if she denied it, Lucy would tell people the real reason she had so much trouble in school. Having a reputation as a slut hadn't been half as bad as the school knowing about her LD.

She ducked out a door and into the cool night air, walking toward the football field situated next to the main building. Two streetlights glowed in the darkness as her eyes scanned the shadowy length of the field.

She'd spent so much time here in high school. If she'd been queen of her class, this was her royal court. She'd felt confident on the field in her cheerleading uniform or on the sidelines cheering for Ethan. She'd hated falling back on her looks, but the insecure girl who had nothing else to offer had exploited her one gift as best she could.

Now she breathed in the cool night air and closed her eyes, remembering the familiar smells and sounds.

Her memories here were a long time gone. She was no longer a scared teenager. She had Charlie to protect. She'd made mistakes and was trying her damnedest to make amends for them. There was no way of moving forward without finally confronting her past, once and for all.

Chapter Ten

She took another breath and headed toward the school, determined to hold her head high. She had as much right to return to her high school as anyone.

Once inside, she stopped at the girls' bathroom to sprinkle cold water on her face. When a stall opened and Lucy Peterson stepped out, Julia wondered if she'd actually conjured her.

"Hi, Lucy." The other woman's eyes widened in surprise.

Lucy hadn't changed much since high school. She was still short and full figured, her chest heaving as she adjusted the wire-rimmed glasses on her face.

"Hello, Julia. I didn't expect to see you here. I'm in town for the weekend for my parents' anniversary. Normally I wouldn't be caught dead back in this high school. I live in Chicago. I'm a doctor." Lucy paused for a breath. "I'm babbling."

"What kind of doctor?" Julia asked.

"Molecular biologist."

Julia nodded. Figured. Julia knew better than to compare herself to a genius like Lucy. "That's great."

The two women stared at each other for several long moments. At the same time they blurted, "I'm sorry."

Relief mixed with a healthy dose of confusion made Julia's shoulders sag. "I'm the one who should apologize. I know I was horrible in high school. You were on the top of my list. Not that it matters, but you should know I was jealous of you."

Lucy looked doubtful. "Of me? You were the homecoming queen, prom queen, head cheerleader, and you dated the football captain. I was nobody."

"You were smart."

"I shouldn't have spread that rumor about you." Lucy fiddled with the ring on her left finger. "You weren't a slut."

"There are worse things you could have said about me."

"You weren't stupid, either."

Julia made her voice light. "The grade record would beg to differ."

"I read your file," Lucy said slowly. "It was wrong, but I know you had significant learning disabilities, which means…"

"It means there's something wrong with my brain," Julia finished. "*Stupid* is a much clearer description of my basic problem."

"You must have been pretty clever to have hid it all those years. I'm guessing you still are."

"I cut hair for a living. It's not nuclear science. Or molecular biology."

"That's right. My mom told me you'd taken over the Hairhouse."

"I'm working on it. The loan still needs to go through."

"Are you going to keep the name?"

Julia relaxed a little as she smiled. "I don't think so. 'The Best Little Hairhouse in Brevia' is quite a mouthful."

Lucy returned the smile then pulled at the ends of her hair. "I'm in town until Tuesday. Could you fit me in?"

"You don't hate me?"

Lucy shook her head. "In high school, I thought I was the only one who was miserable. Once I got away from Brevia, I realized lots of kids had problems. We were all just too narcissistic to see it in each other. Some people can't let go of the past. I've moved on, Julia. I'm happy in Chicago. I have a great career and a fantastic husband. I don't even mind visiting my mom a couple times a year, although I avoid the old crowd. I know in my heart they can't hurt me because their opinions don't matter. I don't hate you. You probably did me a favor. You made me determined to escape. Now I can come back on my own terms."

"I'm glad for you, Lucy." Julia checked her mental calendar. She'd trained herself to keep her schedule in her head so she didn't have to rely on a planner or smartphone. "How about eleven on Monday?"

Lucy nodded. "Maybe we could grab lunch after. I may not care too much about certain ladies' opinions but I wouldn't mind seeing their faces if we showed up at Carl's."

"I'd love that."

"I'll see you Monday." With a quick, awkward hug, Lucy hurried out the door.

Julia studied herself in the hazy mirror above the row of bathroom sinks. She felt lighter than she had in years, the weight of her guilt over how she'd treated Lucy finally lifted. One past mistake vanquished, only a hundred more to go.

"She's right, you know." The door to one of the stalls swung open to reveal Lexi Preston.

Julia's shoulders went rigid again. "Eavesdrop much?" She took a step toward Lexi. "I don't suppose you're going to put that conversation on the official record? It didn't make me out to be the deadbeat you're trying to convince the court I am."

"I don't think you're a deadbeat," Lexi said, sounding almost contrite. "You're not stupid, either. But I have to do my job. The Johnsons—"

"They call the shots, right? You do the dirty work for them, digging up damaging information on me and probably countless other family enemies."

"It's not personal." Lexi's voice was a miserable whisper.

Julia felt a quick stab of sympathy before her temper began to boil over. She was always too gullible, wanting to believe people weren't as bad as they seemed. It led to her being taken advantage of on more than one occasion. Not this time, though.

She had to physically restrain herself from grabbing Lexi's crisp button-down and slamming the petite attorney into one of the metal stalls. "How can you say that? You're helping them take my son away from me. My son!" Tears flooded her eyes and she turned away, once again feeling helpless to stop the inevitable outcome.

"I don't want you to lose your son," Lexi said quietly. "If I had my way…" She paused then added, "Hiding who you are and the reasons you did things isn't going to help your case. You're not the one with the big secrets here."

Julia whirled around. "Are the Johnsons hiding something? Do you have information that could help me keep Charlie?"

Lexi shook her head. "I've said too much." She reached

for the door. "You're a good mother, Julia. But you have to believe it."

Julia followed Lexi into the hall, but before she could catch up a loud crash from down the hall distracted her. She heard a round of shouts and her first thought was of Charlie.

Chaos reigned in the gymnasium as people pushed toward the exits. Julia stood on her tiptoes and scanned the crowd, spotting Joe Callahan with his arm around her mother near the bleachers. Vera held Charlie, who was contentedly spooning ice cream into his mouth, oblivious to the commotion.

Julia elbowed her way through the throng of people to Vera and Joe. "Charlie," she said on a breath, and her son launched himself at her.

"Banilla, Mama."

"I see, sweetie." She hugged him tight against her.

"Why is everyone rushing out of here?" She noticed that many older folks, like Joe and Vera, hung back.

"Big fight outside," someone passing by called. "Eddie Kelton caught his wife in the back of their minivan with his best friend."

"He's going to kill him," the man's companion said with a sick laugh. "Someone said Eddie's got a knife."

Julia grimaced. She'd gone to school with Eddie's older brother. "The Keltons are not a stable bunch," she murmured.

Joe patted her shoulder. "Don't worry, hon. Sam will handle it. I'd be out there but I don't want to leave your mom."

"Such a gentleman."

"Sam?" Julia's heart rate quickened. "Why is Sam out there?"

"Because he's the police chief." Vera spoke slowly, as if Julia were a small child.

"He's not on duty. Shouldn't they call a deputy?"

"Cops are never truly off duty," Joe said with a sigh. "But Sammy can take care of himself."

"Eddie Kelton has a knife." Julia practically jumped up and down with agitation. Her palms were sweating and clammy. Sam could take care of himself, but she couldn't stop her anxiety from spilling over. "This isn't part of the evening's entertainment. It's real life."

Joe nodded. "Being the wife of a law-enforcement officer isn't easy." He patted her shoulder again and she wanted to rip his wrist out of the socket. He pulled his hand away as if he could read her mind. "If it will make you feel better, I'll check on him. I may be rusty but I could handle a couple troublemakers in my day."

Vera gave a dreamy sigh. A muscle above Julia's eye began to twitch.

"I bet you were quite a sight," Vera practically purred.

"You know what would make me feel better? If I go and check on him." She sat Charlie on the bleachers. "Stay here with Grandma, okay, buddy?"

"Gramma," Charlie said around a mouthful.

"I'll escort you," Joe said in the same cop tone Julia'd heard Sam use. "If you're okay for a few minutes on your own?" he asked Vera.

"Be a hero," Vera answered, batting her lashes.

Julia thought about arguing but figured he could be useful. "Can you get me to the front?"

"Yes, ma'am."

He took her elbow and, true to his word, guided her through the groups spilling into the parking lot. Was it some kind of police Jedi mind trick that enabled cops to manage throngs of people?

She poked her head through the row of spectators to see Sam between two men, arms out, a finger pointed at each of them.

Eddie Kelton, his wife, Stacey, and a man Julia didn't recognize stood in the parking lot under the lights. The unknown man had his shirt on inside out and his jeans were half zipped. Julia assumed he was the man Stacey had been with. Another telltale sign was the black eye forming above his cheek.

Stacey stood to one side, weeping loudly into her hands.

"For the last time, Eddie, put the knife down." Sam looked as if he'd grown several inches since Julia had seen him minutes earlier. He was broad and strong, every muscle in his body on full alert. A surge of pride flashed through her, along with the nail-biting fear of seeing him in action.

Eddie Kelton couldn't have been more than five foot seven, a wiry strip of a man, aged beyond his years thanks to working in the sun on a local construction crew. His face sported a bloody nose, busted lip and a large scratch above his left eye. Julia gathered he'd been on the losing end of the fight until he'd brandished the six-inch blade jiggling between his fingers.

"That's my woman, Chief." Eddie's arm trembled. "My wife. He's supposed to be my best friend and he had my wife." Eddie's wild gaze switched to Stacey. "How could you do this to me? I loved you."

She let out a wretched sob. "You don't act like you love me. Always down at the bar after work or passed out on the couch." Her eyes darted around the crowd. "I found the adult movies on the computer. I want someone who wants me. Who pays attention to me. Who makes me feel like a woman and not just the housekeeper."

"I loved you," Eddie screamed.

"It was only—" the half-dressed man began.

"Shut up, Jon-o," Eddie and Stacey yelled at the same time.

Eddie slashed the air with his knife.

Sam held his ground.

Julia held her breath.

"Eddie, I know what you're feeling." Sam's voice was a soothing murmur.

"You don't know squat," Eddie spat out, dancing back and forth on the balls of his feet. "I'm going to cut off his junk here and now."

"Don't you threaten my junk," the other man yelled back. "If you were a real man—"

Sam's head whipped around. "Jon Dallas, shut your mouth or I'm going to arrest you for public indecency." He turned back to Eddie. "I do know. A few years ago I walked in on my brother and my fiancée getting busy on the kitchen table."

A collective gasp went up from the crowd and several heads turned toward Julia. "Not me," she whispered impatiently. "His ex."

Sam's gaze never left Eddie, so she had no idea if he realized she was there.

Eddie's bloodshot eyes brimmed with tears. "It gets you right here," he said, thumping his chest with the hand not gripping the knife. "Like she reached in and cut out your heart."

Sam nodded. "You're not going to make anything better with the knife. Drop it and we'll talk about what's next."

"I'm sorry, Eddie." Stacey's voice was so filled with anguish Julia almost felt sorry for her. Except for the small matter that she'd been caught cheating on her husband. "I made a horrible mistake. It didn't mean anything."

"Hey—" Jon-o sputtered.

"I love you, Eddie." Stacey sobbed.

Eddie lowered the knife but Sam didn't relax. "Drop it and kick it to me," he ordered. "She loves you, Eddie."

"I love her, too." Eddie's voice was miserable. "But she cheated."

"We didn't even do it," Stacey called, and Julia wished the woman understood the concept of *too much information.* "He was drunk. Couldn't get it—"

Jon-o took an angry step toward her. "Shut your fat mouth, you liar. I was the best—"

For a second, Sam's attention switched to Jon-o and Stacey. In that instant, Eddie launched himself forward.

He lunged for Jon-o but Sam grabbed his arm. Julia screamed as Eddie stabbed wildly at Sam, who knocked the blade out of the man's hand then slammed him to the ground. Pete Butler, Sam's deputy, rushed forward and tossed Sam a pair of handcuffs before turning his attention to Jon-o, pushing him away from the action.

Stacey melted into a puddle on the ground. "Eddie, no," she whimpered. "Don't put handcuffs on my husband."

Sam got Eddie to his feet.

"Don't worry, honey." Stacey took a step forward. "I'll bail you out. I love you so much."

Tears ran down Eddie's face. "I love you, sugar-buns."

Stacey would have wrapped herself around her husband but Sam held up a hand. "Later, Stacey." Jon-o disappeared into the crowd and Sam yanked Eddie toward Pete. "Put him in the holding cell overnight. He can sober up."

Pete pointed to Sam's shoulder. Sam shook his head, so the deputy led Eddie toward the waiting squad car.

"We're done out here," Sam announced to the crowd. "Everyone head inside. There's a lot more money to be raised tonight."

After a quiet round of applause, people drifted toward

the gymnasium. A couple of men approached Sam, slapping him on the back.

"I told you he'd handle it," Joe said proudly from Julia's side.

"You did." Julia felt rooted to the spot where she stood. Her body felt as though it weighed a thousand pounds. She couldn't explain what she'd felt when Eddie had rushed at Sam with the knife. She'd swear she'd aged ten years in those few seconds.

"Nice going, son," Joe called.

Sam looked up and his gaze met Julia's. He gave her a small smile and her whole body began to shake. She walked toward him and threw her arms around his neck, burying her face in his shirt collar. He smelled sweet, like leftover cotton candy, and felt so undeniably strong, she could have wept. She wouldn't cry. She wasn't that much of an emotional basket case, but she squeezed her eyes shut for good measure.

She willed the trembling to stop. It started to as he rubbed his palm against her back.

"Hey," he said into her hair. "Not that I'm complaining about you wrapped around me, but it's okay. It was nothing. Eddie was too drunk to do any real damage, even if he'd wanted to."

She didn't know how long he held her. She was vaguely aware of people milling about, of Joe watching from nearby. Sam didn't seem in any hurry to let her go. She needed the strength of his body around hers to reassure her that he was truly all right.

When she was finally in control enough to open her eyes, she was shocked to see blood staining his shirt near the shoulder. "You're hurt." Her voice came out a croak.

He shook his head. "The blade nicked me. It's a scratch.

I'll stop by the hospital after we finish the paperwork to have it cleaned. Nothing more."

"He could have hurt you," she whispered, unable to take her eyes off his shoulder.

He tipped up her chin. His eyes were warm on hers, kind and understanding. "I'm okay. Nothing happened."

"It could have. Every day something *could* happen to you, Sam. Drug busts, drunken fights and who knows what else."

"I'm fine."

"I'm not. I can't stand knowing you're always at risk."

He looked over her shoulder to where Joe stood. When his eyes met hers again, they were cold and unreadable. He leaned in close to her ear. "Then it's a good thing this is a fake engagement. I'm not giving up my life for a woman."

Julia felt the air rush from her lungs. "I didn't say I wanted you to." She grabbed on to the front of his shirt as he moved to pull away. "I know this is fake. Sue me, but I was worried. Heaven forbid someone cares about you, Sam. Expects something from you. Maybe I shouldn't have—"

"Forget it." Sam kissed her cheek, but she knew it was because his father was still watching. "I have to go into the station and then to the hospital, so I'll be a while. Take Charlie home. We'll talk tomorrow."

"Don't do this," she whispered as he walked away, climbing into the police cruiser without looking back.

She knew this was fake. Because she'd never be stupid enough to fall in love with a man so irritating, annoying and unwilling to have a meaningful conversation about his feelings.

She turned to Joe. "At least he's okay. That's most important, right?"

"It's hard for him to be needed by someone," Joe said,

taking her arm and leading her back toward the high school.

Julia snorted. "Ya think?"

Rotating his shoulder where the nurse had cleaned his wound, Sam stepped out of the E.R. into the darkness. His father's car wasn't in front, so he sat on the bench near the entrance to wait.

He scrubbed his palms against his face, wondering how he'd made such a colossal mess of a night that had started off so well. Julia had looked beautiful, as always, and they'd had fun with Charlie at the carnival. He'd even survived his dad and her mother meeting and almost felt okay about her relationship with Ethan.

Then he'd put his foot in his mouth in a thousand different ways when she'd been concerned about his job. Hell, he couldn't name a cop's wife who didn't worry. He'd liked that she'd been worried, liked the feeling of being needed. It had also scared him and he'd pushed her away.

Like he pushed everyone away.

He was alone. Again. As always.

"Need a lift, Chief?"

He turned to see her standing a few feet away, the light from the hospital's entrance making her glow like an angel. Not that he knew whether angels glowed. He imagined they'd want to, if it meant they'd look like Julia Morgan.

"My dad's coming to get me. Where's Charlie?"

"He's having a sleepover with Grandma." She walked to the bench and sat next to him. "How's your shoulder?"

He shrugged, finding it difficult to concentrate with her thigh pressed against his leg. "Hurts worse after the nurse messed with it than when the knife grazed me."

She bit her lip when he said the word *knife*. "You're lucky it wasn't worse."

"I guess."

"Joe's not coming to get you."

"I may want to reconsider that ride."

"You may."

"Why are you here, Julia?"

She rocked back far enough to stuff her fingers under her legs. Lucky fingers. He'd give anything to trade places with her hands.

"Just because our engagement isn't real doesn't mean I can't worry about you. I'm human. I like you. Caring about friends is what people do."

"We're friends." He tried the word out in his mind and decided he liked it. Sam didn't have many real friends.

"I think so."

He couldn't resist asking, "With benefits?"

She continued to stare straight ahead but one side of her mouth kicked up. "That remains to be seen. You're not moving in the right direction with the bad 'tude earlier."

"Would it help if I said I was sorry?"

"Are you?"

With one finger, he traced a path down her arm, gently tugging on her wrist until she lifted her hand. He intertwined his fingers with hers. "Yes, I'm sorry. I'm sorry you were scared. I'm sorry I was a jerk."

"I know you don't owe me anything."

"I do owe you. So far, I'm the only one who's benefited from our arrangement. You wouldn't let me go to court with you. I made an enormous mess of trying to get your mind off the case and now you're here picking me up. What have I done to help you? Nothing."

"That's not true."

"It is. I want to help. I'm going to the final hearing with you."

"I—"

"No arguments."

She nodded. That was a start. "We can get people to submit affidavits on your behalf," he continued. "Character references for you. The girls from the salon will do it. I bet Ida Garvey would, too, now that her hair isn't bright pink. I want to hear you agree. I can help. You have to let me."

"My LD changes everything." She looked at him, her eyes fierce. He knew this moment meant something big.

"You have trouble reading," he said slowly. "And with numbers. It caused a lot of problems but you told me you're working with a specialist."

"My brain doesn't work right." She made the statement with conviction, as if daring him to disagree.

"Is that the clinical diagnosis? Your brain doesn't work right? I don't think so, sweetie."

"Don't 'sweetie' me. I'm stupid, and Jeff and his family know it. My brain is broken. It takes me twice as long as it should to read a simple letter. Why do you think I bring paperwork home from the salon so often? I spend all night checking and rechecking my work so I don't make mistakes."

"Everyone makes mistakes."

"You don't understand. But Jeff does. He knows how badly I want this to stay a secret." She bolted up from the bench, pacing back and forth in front of him. "So much of what the attorney is talking about stems from my LD. I've hidden it for years and now they're using it against me."

"Why keep it a secret?"

"Because—" she dragged out the word on a ragged breath "—if the people around me knew how dumb I am, they could and would take advantage of me. In Brevia, I can hide it. If I really get into a bind, my mom or Lainey can help. I don't want the whole town talking about it."

Something struck a chord deep within Sam. He knew

what it was like to put on a mask so people couldn't really see what was inside of you. He knew how it felt to be afraid you wouldn't measure up. But his demons were more easily buried than Julia's. The thought of how much time and energy she'd put into hiding this piece of herself made his heart ache.

She was smart, proud and brave. She'd spent years making everyone believe she didn't care, when the reality was that she cared more than she could admit. He could see it on her face, see the tension radiating through her body as she waited for him to judge her the way she'd been judging herself for years.

He stood and cupped her face between his hands. "You're not stupid."

She searched his eyes, as if willing the words to be true. "They're trying to use it against me, Sam. To prove that Charlie would be better off with them. Not only are they ready to lavish him with their version of lifestyles of the rich and famous, they're saying that if he has the same disorder..." Her voice caught and she bit her lip before continuing, "If I've given this to him, they have the resources to get him the best help."

"*You* are what's best for him." He used his thumb to wipe away a lone tear that trailed down her cheek then brought his lips to the spot, tasting the salt on her skin.

The automatic doors slid open and a hospital worker pushed a wheelchair into the night.

"Let's get out of here," Sam whispered.

Julia nodded, and he cradled her against him as they walked to her car.

"Let me drive," he said when she reached into her purse for the keys.

"You're the injured one." But when he took the keys from her hand, she didn't argue.

The streets were quiet. Julia didn't speak, but she held on to the hand he placed in her lap. He could imagine the thoughts running through her mind as she realized the secret she'd held close for so long was about to become public. She was wrung out emotionally, and he hated seeing it. All he wanted was to make her feel better, if only for a few moments.

He pulled into his driveway and turned off the ignition.

"I should go home," she said, releasing his fingers. "You need to rest."

Rest was the last thing on Sam's mind. He might not be a master with words but he knew he wasn't going to let her go tonight. If he couldn't tell her how amazing she was and have her believe it, he could damn well show her.

He came around to open her car door and draw her out, lacing his fingers with hers once again.

"I need to go," she repeated, her voice small.

Without a word, he led her up onto the porch and unlocked his front door. He turned and pulled her to him, slanting his mouth over hers. For a moment she froze, then she melted against him, the spark between them flaring into an incendiary fire.

He kissed her jaw and the creamy skin of her throat, whispering, "Stay with me."

She nodded as he nipped at her earlobe and, not letting her go, reached back to push open the door and drag them both through. He kicked it shut and tugged on the hem of her T-shirt.

"This. Off. Now."

"Bossy," she said breathlessly. Through his desire, he heard the confidence return to her tone and was so glad for it, he could have laughed out loud.

Just as suddenly, he couldn't make a sound as she pulled the soft cotton over her head and was left bathed in moonlight wearing only a lacy black bra and jeans slung low on her hips.

Sweet mercy.

He knew she was beautiful, but he'd been with beautiful women before. Watching her watch him, though, her eyes smoky and wanting, was almost his undoing.

He flicked one thin strap off her shoulder, then the other, not quite exposing her completely but giving him a view of more creamy flesh. He traced the line of fabric across the tops of her breasts and his body grew heavy at her intake of breath.

She wrapped her hand around his finger and lifted it to her mouth, kissing the tip softly. "You, now," she commanded, her voice husky.

Sam was happy to comply, and he threw his shirt onto the nearby couch. She stepped forward and, in one fluid motion, reached behind her to unhook her bra. It fell to the floor between them. Then she pressed herself against his chest and trailed her lips over his wounded shoulder.

"If it matters," he said, his voice hoarse, "that's not the part that hurts."

He felt her smile against him. "We'll get to that. All in good time, Chief. All in good time."

From Sam's point of view, that time was now. He bent his head and took her mouth, kissing her as he reached between them to unfasten her jeans. He dropped to his knees in front of her, kissing the curve of her belly. She smelled like sin and sunshine, and the mix made him dizzy with need.

"I want you, Julia Morgan." He lifted his head so he could look into her eyes. "I want you," he repeated. "All of you. Just the way you are."

Her lips parted, and he saw trust and vulnerability flash in her eyes. He wanted that, wanted all of this. For the first time in his life, he wanted to be a man someone could depend on for the long haul.

He wanted to be a real hero.

"I'm going to take care of you," he whispered.

She smiled at him and shimmied her hips so that her jeans slipped off them.

"What are you waiting for?" she asked, and he straightened, capturing her mouth again.

Sam broke the kiss long enough to lead her the few steps to the couch. He stripped off his jeans then eased his body over hers, relishing the feel of skin on skin. She fit perfectly under him, as he'd guessed she would.

He savored every touch, taking the time to explore her body with his fingers and mouth. Her answering passion filled him with a desire he'd never imagined before tonight. He finally made her his, entering her with an exquisite slowness before his need for her took over and they moved together in a perfect rhythm.

"You are amazing," he whispered as he held her gaze.

"You're not so bad yourself," she answered, but her eyes were cloudy with passion.

"I'm going to prove how very good I am." He smiled then nipped at the soft skin of her earlobe. "All night long."

Chapter Eleven

Wow.

Hours later, Julia's brain registered that one syllable.

"Wow," Sam murmured against her hair, clearly still trying to catch his breath.

She knew the feeling. She'd had good sex in her life—maybe even great a couple of times. This night had blown away her every expectation about what intimacy felt like when it was exactly right. She wanted to believe it was because she'd been on a long hiatus.

If she admitted the truth, Sam had been worth a two-year wait. Her body felt boneless, as if she never wanted to move from where she lay stretched across him, the short hair on his chest tickling her bare skin.

The unfamiliar feeling of contentment jolted her back into reality. Their relationship was precarious enough, sometimes hot and often cold enough to give her frost-bite. He challenged her, irritated her and filled her with such incredible need, she wondered how she'd walk away when the business part of their arrangement was over.

That sobering thought in mind, she rolled off him. He automatically tucked the light duvet in around her. They'd made it to his bedroom.

Eventually.

After the couch in his living room. And the stairs. The stairs? She hadn't even known that was possible, let alone that it would be downright amazing.

It was still dark and she couldn't make out much more than the outlines of furniture around the room and the fact that his bed was enormous. It suited him.

She glanced at the glowing numbers of the digital clock on the nightstand next to the bed. He shifted, propping himself on one elbow and wrapping the other arm around her waist.

"Don't go."

She tilted her head away, his face in shadow from the moonlight slanting through the bedroom window. She couldn't see his eyes and hoped hers were hidden, as well.

How did he know she was getting ready to bolt? Julia had never been much of a cuddler. The emotional boundaries she put around herself often manifested in physical limits, as well.

She looked at the ceiling. Even if she couldn't see his eyes, she knew his gaze was intense. "As fun as this was…"

His soft chuckle rumbled in the quiet, making her insides tingle again. She'd done a lot of tingling tonight.

"Fun," he repeated.

"We've got chemistry."

He laughed again.

"This isn't funny." She didn't want to make more of this than it was. She'd start talking and end up embarrassing herself with romantic declarations about how much she liked—more than liked, if she admitted the truth—being with Sam, both in the bedroom and out of it. He was the first man she felt wanted her for her, not what she looked like or an image she portrayed. It was both liberating and frightening to reveal her true self to someone.

"*You're* funny." He kissed the tip of her nose and pulled her tighter against the length of him. "And smart." He kissed one cheek. "And sexy as hell." Then the other. "I want you to spend the night." His lips met hers.

She broke the kiss. "I think we've about wrapped things up here."

He traced the seam of her mouth with his tongue. "We've only gotten started."

Julia felt her resolve disappear. She knew it was a mistake but she couldn't make her body move an inch. "Are you sure?"

"I've never been more sure."

It had been ages since Julia'd wanted to be with someone as much as she did Sam. "I guess that would be okay."

"Okay?" He tickled her belly and she wriggled in response.

"More than okay."

"That's what I thought."

She expected him to kiss her again, but instead he snuggled in behind her, smoothing her hair across the pillow.

"Sleep," he told her.

"Oh. I thought you wanted to…"

"I do. Later."

Her spine stiffened. "I've never been much for spooning."

"I can tell." His finger drew circles along her back until she began to relax. "Why did you pick me up tonight?"

"I don't like pillow talk, either," she muttered, and he laughed again.

He didn't press her for more, just continued to trace patterns along her skin. The silence was companionable, the room still and soft in the night. She stretched her head against the pillow, relishing the feeling of being surrounded by Sam. His scent lingered in the sheets, the combination of outdoors and spice that continued to make her head spin.

"Okay," she said after a few minutes, "I kind of get why all those women were hung up on you."

"What women?"

She lightly jabbed her elbow into his stomach. "Your Three Strikes Sam fan club. You're pretty good at this stuff."

"Only with you."

"I don't believe that."

"No changing the subject. I was a jerk tonight. You gave me another chance. Thank you."

She took a deep breath. "I can use all the help I can get. There's no use hiding it."

"You shouldn't hide anything," he said softly.

"I saw Lexi Preston at the carnival."

"Your ex's attorney?"

"She was there checking up on me, I think. Lots of stories to be dished from my former frenemies." She gave a sad laugh. "Lexi thinks they wouldn't be so hard on me now if they'd known what I was dealing with back then."

"Maybe you wouldn't be so hard on yourself if you told the truth," Sam suggested.

"Could be," she said with a yawn. It had been a long day. A light shiver ran through her and he pulled her closer. "Good Lord, you're a furnace." She snuggled in closer. "My own personal space heater."

"Whatever you need me to be," Sam agreed.

That was the last thing Julia heard him say before she drifted off to sleep.

She woke a few hours later and they made love again in the hazy predawn light. His eyes never left hers as they moved together, and Julia knew this night changed what was between them, even if they both acted as though it didn't.

She'd wanted him since the first time she'd laid eyes on him, no matter how much she tried to deny it. Now that she knew how good it could be, she wasn't sure how she'd ever adjust back to real life. She had to, she reminded herself, even as she snuggled in closer to him. This night was a fringe benefit of their business arrangement, and if she let herself forget that, she knew she'd lose her heart along the way.

"You're finally ready to get back into action?"

Sam ripped open a sugar packet and dumped it into his coffee. "I haven't been sitting on a beach sipping fruity drinks for the past couple of years."

"You know what I mean."

He watched his brother shovel another bite of pancakes into his mouth. Scott always could eat like a horse. Not that Scott was a kid anymore. He was twenty-nine and a good two inches taller than Sam's six feet. They both had the Callahan blue eyes and linebacker build, but Scott had their mother's olive coloring and dark hair. Sometimes a look or gesture from Scott could bring back a memory of their mom so vividly it was as if she was still with them.

"I'm glad you called me." Scott downed the rest of his orange juice and signaled the waitress for another. "I felt real bad about what happened."

"About having sex with my fiancée?"

Scott flinched. "Pretty much. Although you have to know by now I wasn't the first."

Sam gave a curt nod. "I'm still not going to thank you, if that's what you're getting at."

"I'm not."

"I didn't come here to talk about Jenny or rehash the past."

"Dad called last week. He told me you're engaged again."

Sam looked out the window of the café into the sunny morning. He'd met Scott in a town halfway between Brevia and D.C., far enough away that he wouldn't see any familiar faces. It had been almost a week since the night of the carnival. He'd seen Julia and Charlie almost every day. Sometimes it was under the guise of making their relationship look real. He'd taken them to lunch and to a neighboring playground, stopped by the salon when he had a break during the day.

He was happiest when it was just the three of them. He'd pick up dinner after his shift, or she'd cook and they'd take the dog for a walk, and then he'd help get Charlie ready for bed. They agreed if he was going to be a presence at the mediation or future court dates, it would be smart for Charlie to feel comfortable with him.

Sam hadn't expected how much playing family would fill up the empty parts of him. He counted the hours each day until he could lift Charlie in his arms and even more the moments until he could pull Julia to him.

He took another drink of coffee then answered, "It's complicated. But I'm engaged."

Complicated might be the understatement of the century where Julia was concerned. She'd opened up to him and shared her deepest secret. She trusted him with her son, her dreams for the future, and it scared him to death. He steered their conversations away from the topic of his work, no matter how often she asked about details of his day.

After the scene at the carnival, he didn't want to see

worry in her gaze or argue about the risks he took. It reminded him too much of his parents. Even so, he knew he was going to go through hell when their arrangement was finished. He'd called Scott last week and set up this meeting to talk about a new job away from Brevia, but now his purpose was twofold.

"I need some information on a family from Ohio, very prominent in the area. Dennis and Maria Johnson."

"What kind of information?" Scott asked.

"Whatever you've got. My fiancée, Julia, has a kid with their son and they're making waves with the current custody arrangement. They've got a lot of money and influence and are pulling out the stops to make her life hell. From my experience, people who want to throw their weight around like that have done it before. I'm guessing they have some skeletons from past skirmishes. I want to know what they are."

Scott nodded. "I've got a couple of friends up there. I'll make a call, see what I can find out." He stabbed another bite of pancake then pointed his fork at Sam. "This Julia must be special. You always play by the rule book. It's not like you to fight dirty."

"I'm fighting to win. There's too much at stake not to."

"I'd like to meet her."

Sam felt his whole body tense. His voice lowered to a controlled growl. "Stay away from her, Scott. She isn't like Jenny."

Scott held up his hands, palms up. "I get it. I get it."

The waitress brought a second juice and refilled Sam's coffee. Scott winked at her and she practically tripped backing away from the table.

Sam wanted to roll his eyes. "I see you haven't changed. Still chasing tail all over the place?"

"Why mess with a system that works so damn well? I'm

happy. The ladies are happy. All good. I wasn't cut out for commitment." He lifted one eyebrow. "Until I got Dad's call, I would have guessed you weren't, either."

"Dad thinks love makes the world go round."

"Dad's gone soft and it gives me the creeps."

"Amen to that."

"When you texted, you asked about openings at headquarters." Scott had worked for the U.S. Marshals Service since he'd gotten out of the army.

Sam took a drink of coffee. "You got anything?" It had been easy to imagine a future in Brevia when he'd only been the police chief, before it had started to really feel like home. Before Julia.

Scott nodded. "Maybe, but I don't get it. Why do you want to look at a new job if you're getting married? Being a cop is tough enough on a relationship. The Marshals Service would be the kiss of death. What we do doesn't compute with the minivan lifestyle."

"I told you, it's complicated."

"You're gonna run," Scott said, his voice quiet.

"I'm not running anywhere." Sam felt pressure build behind his eyes. Despite being younger, wild and reckless, Scott always had an uncanny ability to read Sam. It drove him nuts. "You said yourself the Callahans aren't meant for commitment. It may be a matter of time before she sees that. It'll be easier on us both if I'm not around for the fallout."

Scott nodded. "That's more like the brother I know and love. For a minute I thought Dad had brainwashed you with all his hug-it-out bull. Do you know he called my boss to see if he could do a seminar on using emotional intelligence in the field?"

"What's emotional intelligence?"

"Beats me," Scott said with a shrug. "But I'm sure as

hell not interested in finding out. Did you fill out the paper-work I sent you?"

Sam slid an envelope across the table. "It's got my résumé with it."

"We'd be lucky to have you," Scott said solemnly. "I'd be honored to work together."

Sam's phone buzzed, alerting him that he had a voice-mail message. Coverage was spotty in this area, so he wasn't sure when the call had come in. He looked at his phone and saw six messages waiting.

"We did have some good times," he admitted as he punched the keypad to retrieve them. He wasn't on duty, so he couldn't imagine why anyone would need him so urgently.

"Here's to many more." Scott lifted his juice glass in a toast.

Sam listened to the first message and felt the blood drain from his face. He stood, tossing a twenty on the table. "I need to go."

"Everything okay?" Scott asked, mopping up syrup with his last bite of pancake.

Sam was already out the door.

Chapter Twelve

Sam was about forty-five minutes from Brevia. He made it to the hospital in less than thirty.

"Charlie Morgan," he said to the woman at the front desk of the E.R., and she pointed to a room halfway down the hall. He stopped to catch his breath then pushed open the door.

A nurse stood talking to Julia as Vera held Charlie in her lap on the bed. A bright blue cast covered the boy's left wrist.

All three women looked up as Sam walked in. Julia stood so stiff he imagined she might crack in half if he touched her. The urge to ease some of her worry engulfed him.

"Sam," Charlie said, a little groggily, waving his casted arm.

"Hey, buddy." Sam came forward and bent down in front of the boy. "I like your new super arm."

Charlie giggled softly and reached out for Sam to hold him. Vera's eyes widened but she let Sam scoop him up. With Charlie in his arms, he turned to Julia.

"Are you okay?" he asked, wrapping his free arm around her shoulders.

She nodded but remained tense. "The nurse is giving me discharge papers. We've been here for over two hours." Her eyes searched his. "I couldn't reach you."

"I'm sorry," he said simply. "I was out of cell range."

She looked as if she wanted to say more but the nurse cleared her throat. "I've got instructions on bathing him with the cast," she said, holding out a slip of paper. "Take a look and let me know if you have questions."

Gingerly, Julia took the piece of paper. She stared at it, her forehead puckering as her mouth tightened into a thin, frustrated line.

Vera rose to stand beside him. Julia looked up and met his gaze, her eyes miserable. He tugged the paper from her fingers. "Why don't you go over what we need to do?" he said to the nurse. "Just to be on the safe side. We'll take the instructions home, too."

As the woman explained the procedure, Sam felt Vera squeeze his shoulder. "Thank you," she whispered then slipped out of the room.

When the nurse finished her explanation, Julia asked a couple of questions, and then the woman left them alone. Charlie's head drooped on Sam's shoulder and his eyes drifted shut.

"I can take him," Julia said, holding out her hands but keeping her gaze focused on her son.

"I've got him." Sam tipped her chin up so she had to look him in the eye. "I'm sorry, Jules. I'm sorry I wasn't here."

"You don't owe us anything." She picked up the diaper bag from the chair next to the bed. "I want to go home."

Sam followed her into the hall and toward the elevator. She didn't say a word until they were in the parking lot. "I shouldn't have called you. We're not your problem." She took Charlie and settled him in the car seat.

"I'm sorry," Sam said again. A warm breeze played with the ends of her hair. Spring was in full swing in the Smoky Mountains. He wondered how old Charlie needed to be to hold a tiny fishing rod. There were so many things he wanted to do with her and Charlie before their time together ended. Before she figured out she should have never depended on him in the first place. He couldn't stand the thought that today might be the first nail in his coffin. "I know you were scared. I wish I had been here earlier."

She jerked her head in response and he saw tears fill her eyes. "I put the toy car together—one of those ones a toddler pushes around." She swiped at her cheeks. "I swear I followed the directions, but when he knocked it against the kitchen table, it fell apart. Charlie went down over it and landed on his arm. His scream was the worst sound I've ever heard."

Sam wrapped his arms around her. "It was an accident. Not your fault."

She let him hold her but stayed ramrod straight, obviously trying to manage her fear and anxiety. "It *was* my fault. I'm sure I read the directions wrong and Charlie got hurt because of it. Because of me!"

She yanked away from him, pacing next to the car. "Maybe the Johnsons are doing the right thing." Her eyes searched his. "I felt like an idiot when the nurse gave me his discharge papers. Do you know how long it takes me to figure out the right dose of medicine for him? How many things I have to memorize and hope I don't mess up? He's still a baby, Sam. What's going to happen when he gets into school and needs help with his homework? When he wants me to read real books to him? He's going to know his mother is stupid."

"Stop it." Sam grabbed her wrists and pulled her to him, forcing her to look up at him. "Learning disabilities don't make you stupid."

"You don't know how people have looked at me my whole life. It will kill me if Charlie someday looks at me like that." She took a deep, shuddering breath and Sam felt the fight go out of her.

"He's not going to, Julia. He's going to see you like I do. Like your family does. Like a brave, intelligent, fearless woman who doesn't let anything hold her back."

"Really?" She gave him a sad smile. "Because I don't see anyone around here who fits your description." She shrugged out of his embrace and opened the door of her car. "I need to get him home. Thanks for coming, Sam."

"I'll meet you at your apartment."

"You don't need to—"

"I'm going to pick up dinner and a change of clothes and I'll be there within the hour. For once, don't argue with me. Please."

She nodded. "Nice touch with the *please*."

He watched her drive away then headed to his own car. He had to make Julia see how much she had to offer her son. That was the key to her winning the custody battle, no matter what crazy accusations her ex-boyfriend's family threw out. If he could make her believe in herself, he knew she was strong enough to overcome any odds.

She'd win and he'd get the hell out of her life. His heart was lacking what it took to give her the life she deserved. He knew for certain that if she got too close to him, he'd only hurt her and Charlie. Just like he had today.

Sam was like a tin man, without a real heart. He might have been born with one but it had shriveled into nothing when his mother died. He couldn't risk loving and being hurt like that again.

Julia was standing over Charlie's crib when the doorbell rang. Casper growled softly from his place next to her.

"No bark," she whispered, amazed at how the dog seemed to know to keep quiet while Charlie was asleep.

She padded to the door.

"How's Charlie?" Sam asked when she opened it.

She nodded and stepped back. "Sleeping soundly."

Casper gave Sam a full-tooth grin and wagged his stubby tail. "No home for this guy yet?" Sam asked, reaching down to scratch behind the dog's ears. "You need to learn to keep your choppers hidden, buddy."

"I'm adopting him."

Sam's eyebrows rose. "Kind of a small place for a big dog."

"Charlie loves him." She didn't want to admit how much of her decision was based on her need to make something work, even if it was rescuing a stray animal. She took the carryout bag from his hand and turned for the kitchen.

Sam grabbed her around the waist and pulled her against him. "You've got a sharp tongue but a soft heart," he whispered against her ear.

"Wicked elbow, too," she said and jabbed him in the stomach.

He grunted a laugh and released her. "Why is it you don't want people to see how much you care?"

She busied herself pulling plates out of the cabinet. "I care about Charlie. That's enough for me."

"Ida Garvey told me you volunteered to do hair for the middle-school dance team's competition next month."

"Did you see those girls last year? It was updo à la light socket. I know Southerners love big hair but jeez." She set the table and took out the food. "Is this from Carl's?"

"Double burgers with cheese. Hope you approve."

"Perfect."

"I also heard you go to the retirement home once a week and do the ladies' hair."

She shrugged. "A lot of those gals were once customers at the Hairhouse, and their daughters and granddaughters still are. It's good for my business."

"It's because you care."

Why was Sam giving her the third degree on her volunteer hours? "You're making too much of it. I do things that benefit me. Ask anyone around here. I have a long history of being in it for myself."

"That's what you want people to believe."

"That *is* what they believe." She picked up a fry and pointed it at him, feeling her temper starting to rise. "What does it matter?"

He folded himself into the seat across from her. "I want you to understand you're not alone. You have a community here that would rally around you if you gave them a chance."

She took a bite of burger, her eyes narrowing. What the hell did Sam Callahan know about her part in this community? "Are you seriously giving me a lecture on letting people in, Mr. I-am-a-rock-I-am-an-island? You could take your own advice."

He frowned. "I'm a part of this community."

"No, you're not. You circle around the perimeter and insert yourself when someone needs a helping hand. No one really understands how much you give or the toll it takes on you. You're always 'on.' You're terrified of being alone with your empty soul, so you spend a little time with a woman. You get her to fall in love with you so you can hold on to the affection without having to offer any in return. People know what kind of cookies you like, so their single daughters can bake you a batch. But you're as closed off as I am in your own way."

He got up from the table so quickly she thought he was going to storm out. Instead, he grabbed two beers from her fridge, opened them and handed one to her. "We're quite a pair," he said softly, clinking the top of his bottle against hers. "Both so damned independent we'd rather fake an engagement than actually deal with real feelings."

"It's better that way," she answered and took a long drink.

"I used to think so," he said, and his eyes were so intense on hers she lost her breath for a moment. "Do you ever wonder what it would feel like to let someone in?"

She didn't need to because she already had, with him.

Oh, no. Where had that thought come from?

It was true. Without realizing it or intending to, Julia had let Sam not only into her life but into her heart, as well.

She was in love with him.

She stood, gripping the edge of the counter as if it was the only solid thing in her world. She'd called him today when Charlie had gotten hurt before she'd even called her mother. She loved him and she needed him. Julia didn't know which scared her more.

They had a deal, and she was pretty sure Sam was the type of guy who kept his word. He'd help her get through the custody battle as much as he could, but that didn't mean… It didn't mean what her heart wanted it to.

"I don't have room to let anyone in but Charlie," she said in the most casual tone she could muster. "There's not enough of me left for anyone else to hold on to. Everything I can give belongs to him."

"I never had that much to begin with," Sam said from the table.

When Julia felt as if she could turn around without revealing her true emotions, she smiled at him. "That's why we're a perfect match. Hollow to the core."

Sam tossed her a sexy smile. "I know a good way to fill the void."

She tried to ignore the flash of electricity that raced along her spine at the suggestion in his words. "It's been a long day."

He stood and she wrapped her arms around her waist. "Really long."

"It could be an even longer night if you play your cards right."

She couldn't help the grin that spread across her face. "The only game I play is Old Maid."

"I'll teach you."

"No, thanks."

He reached out his hand, palm up, but didn't touch her. "You want to be alone tonight? Say the word and I'll go. I'm not going to push you." One side of his mouth quirked. "No matter how much you want me to."

She shut her eyes, a war raging inside of her. Letting him go was the smart thing to do, the best way to protect what little hold she still had on her heart.

"Tell me to go, Julia."

"Stay," she whispered and found herself enveloped in his arms, his mouth pressed hard on hers. Their tongues mingled and she let her hands slide up his back, underneath his shirt, reveling in the corded muscles that tightened at her touch.

"You feel like heaven," he said as he trailed kisses along her throat, her skin igniting hotter at every touch.

"Bedroom," she said on a ragged breath. "Now."

She gave a small squeak as he lifted her into his arms as if she weighed nothing. It felt good to be swept off her feet, even for the few moments he carried her down the hall.

She glanced at the door to Charlie's room. She hadn't had a man in her bed since she'd gotten pregnant with her son. It felt new and strange.

"It's going to be a challenge," Sam whispered.

"What?"

"Keeping you quiet with what I have planned."

"Oh." Her heart skipped a beat at the promise in his voice.

He laid her across the bed then followed her down, kissing her until her senses spun with desire.

"Too many clothes." She tugged on his shirt.

He stood, pulling the T-shirt over his head and shrugging out of his faded cargo shorts. Julia's breath caught again. His body was perfect, muscles rippling—actually rippling—as he bent forward and caught the waistband of her shorts with two fingers. She lifted herself to meet him as he undressed her, sliding his soft fingers across her skin.

She tried to speed their pace but Sam wouldn't have it, taking his time to explore every inch of her. He murmured endearments against her flesh, making it impossible for her to keep her emotions out of the equation.

When he finally entered her, Julia practically hummed with desire. They moved together, climbing to the highest peaks of ecstasy.

Later, as he held her, she tried to convince herself that it was only a physical connection, but her heart burned for him as much as her body did.

When she finally woke, light poured through the curtains. Julia glanced at the clock then bounded out of bed and across the hall. Charlie never slept past seven and it was already nine-thirty. Panic gripped her.

Her son's crib was empty. She heard voices in the kitchen and took a deep breath. Sam sat at the table next to Charlie's high chair, giving him spoonfuls of oatmeal.

Charlie waved his sippy cup when he saw her, squealing with delight. Casper trotted up, another big grin spread across his face.

Julia noticed the two paper coffee cups on the counter.

Sam followed her gaze. "We took the dog out to do his business and grabbed coffee and muffins. Charlie picked blueberry for you."

She dropped a kiss on Charlie's forehead. "How do you feel, sweet boy?" she asked, and he babbled a response to her. Her fingers brushed over the cast on his arm, but he didn't seem bothered by it. She sent up a silent prayer of thanks that he was okay.

She turned to Sam, who looked rumpled, sleepy and absolutely irresistible as he stirred the soupy oatmeal with a plastic spoon. "What time did he get up?"

"I heard him talking to himself around sunrise-thirty," he said with a smile.

Julia grimaced. "He's an early riser. You should have woken me."

"You were sleeping soundly. I figure you don't get too many mornings off, so…"

"Thanks." She leaned down to kiss him, and he pulled her between his thighs into a quick hug. "For everything. This morning and last night."

"More," Charlie yelled, and Sam shifted so he could give the boy another bite.

Julia stepped to the counter and took a long drink of coffee, and then she dug in the bag for a muffin.

This was too easy, she thought, as she watched Sam make faces at Charlie while he fed him, her son laughing and playing peekaboo with his cup. It felt too right. This was what she wanted, for Charlie and for herself. A family. This was what she'd never have with Sam. He'd made it clear to her that he didn't want a family. Now or ever. The thought was like a swift kick to her gut.

"I should get ready," she said, realizing her tone must have been too harsh when he glanced at her, a question in his eyes.

"I can stay while you shower," he offered.

She wanted to refuse. She knew she should push him out of her house and her life before it became harder to think of letting him go. But that would give too much away. Whether it was Old Maid or some other game, Julia did one thing well: playing her cards close to the vest.

"That would be great." She headed for the bathroom. By the time she was out, Sam had dressed, made her bed and cleaned up the kitchen. Charlie sat watching *Sesame Street,* cuddled with Casper on the couch as Sam leaned against the back of it.

"When is the next meeting?"

She sighed. "Two days from now."

"I'll drive with you."

She nodded, unable to put into words what that meant to her.

"My dad left a message this morning. He wants to take us to dinner tonight."

"I can do that."

"Along with your mom."

"Uh-oh."

"You can say that again. If those two are plotting…"

"Do you think they suspect anything?"

He shook his head. "They want to talk about wedding plans."

Julia's stomach lurched. "That's bad."

Sam pushed away from the couch. "We'll make it work. We've come this far."

He brushed his lips against hers, a soft touch but it still made her stomach quiver. "Five-thirty. Do you want me to pick you up?"

"I'll have to get Charlie from the sitter's first. I'll meet you there."

He kissed her again. "Have a good day, Julia."

He made those five little words sound like a caress.

"You, too," she muttered and stepped back.

"I'll see you later, buddy." Sam bent and ruffled Charlie's hair, the gesture so natural Julia felt herself melt all over again.

Charlie's fist popped out of his mouth. "'Bye, Dada," he said, not taking his eyes from the television.

Sam straightened slowly.

"He didn't mean anything," Julia said with a forced laugh, not wanting to reveal how disconcerted she felt.

"I know," Sam said softly.

"He knows you're not his dad. He doesn't even understand what that word means. It's something he sees on TV. A word for men. It isn't—"

"Julia." He cut her off, his hand chopping through the air. "It's okay."

But it wasn't okay. Sam was spooked. She knew by the way he didn't turn to her again. He lifted his hand to wave, and with a stilted "See you later," he was gone.

Chapter Thirteen

Sam was freaked out. He took another drink of his beer and glanced around the crowd at Carl's, reliving the pure terror he'd felt this morning.

In his career as a police officer, he'd had guns and knives pulled on him, dealt with drug dealers, prostitutes and an assortment of random losers. He didn't lose his cool or let his guard down. The danger and risk of the job never rattled him.

But one word from a toddler had shaken him to his core. Charlie'd called him Dada. Although Julia had tried to play it off, he knew that she was affected by it, too. He'd heard it in her tone. Not that he'd been able to do much talking, afraid his voice would crack under the weight of the conflicting emotions warring inside him.

Sam had never planned on being a father. Even when he'd been engaged to Jenny, neither of them had wanted kids. That was one of the things that had made him propose, even when he'd had the nagging sense something wasn't right in their relationship. It wasn't every day a guy found a woman who wasn't itching to have babies.

Sam liked kids, but he knew he didn't have what it took to be a decent father. He lacked the emotional depth to put someone else's needs before his own. He believed he was incapable of feeling something, much like his own father had been after his mother's death.

Charlie made him want to change, to be a better man.

He loved the feeling of that boy cuddled against him, his small head nestled in the crook of Sam's neck. He loved watching him follow the silly dog around and vice versa. He especially loved seeing Julia with Charlie, how happy it made her to be with her son.

He hadn't understood that bond when Charlie was a newborn. When he'd seen Julia with the small bundle after the boy's birth, Sam had run the other way. Part of him might have known instinctively how much he'd want to be a part of their world.

That was impossible. He could help her fight for her son, but he didn't have any more to give. He understood the look in her eyes when she'd thought he was in danger. He remembered the same fear in his mother's eyes each time the phone rang while his father was on duty. Her fear and worry had eventually turned into resentment.

He wouldn't give up who he was and he couldn't ask Julia to be a part of his life. He wouldn't risk what it could do to her. He knew Julia was stronger than his mother had ever been, but the life of cop's wife could wreck the strongest woman, no two ways about it.

He'd miss her like crazy, though. Already he could feel the loss of the two of them and he wasn't even gone.

"Okay, let's do this." Julia sat down at the table, her

posture rigid. Her eyes darted around as if scoping escape routes. "They're not here yet?"

Sam shook his head. "Did you have a good day?" He reached across the table to take her hand but she snatched it away.

"No use for the small talk. Save it for the audience."

Despite the fact she'd never truly been his, Sam wished for the way it had been before this morning, when she'd been unguarded and happy to be with him. He glanced around at the crowded restaurant. "There's always an audience in Brevia. Where's Charlie?"

"His sitter had an appointment, so I had him at the salon this afternoon. Lainey is watching him tonight. I thought…it's simpler without him here. We should limit the amount of time he spends with you. So that he doesn't get too attached and all." Her eyes flashed, daring him to argue with her. She was in full mama-bear mode tonight. It made him want her all the more.

Sam's gut twisted at the thought of not spending time with Charlie. "He's an amazing boy, Julia."

"He's great," she agreed distractedly. Her fingers played with the napkin on the table.

He gave a short laugh. "I didn't realize how quiet my life was until you came along."

She glanced toward the front of the restaurant. "Where do you think they are? I want to get this over with."

"My dad and your mom are coming to discuss wedding plans. You look like you can't stand to be in the same room as me." He extended his ankle and pressed it against her shin. "Relax."

She snatched her leg away, her knee banging on the underside of the table. She grabbed the water glass before it tumbled over. "I can't relax," she said between clenched teeth. "This whole thing was a mistake. You're in our lives temporarily, and now Charlie is developing feelings for you. It has to end, Sam."

He swallowed the panic rising in his throat. "You don't mean tonight?"

"Why not?" she countered. "The sooner the better."

Hell, no, he screamed inside his head.

"I don't think that's prudent at this time, Julia," he told her, his voice calm and measured. "I don't want Charlie hurt, but our business arrangement is helping all of us in the long run. You're so close to a ruling, and my dad should be heading back to Boston within the week. Stick it out, Jules. I promise it'll be worth it."

"Business arrangement," she repeated softly. "You still consider this a business arrangement?"

Something in the way she looked at him made him uneasy, but she had to know what he meant. He was doing this for her benefit—at least that was what he tried to tell himself.

"We talked about it last night. You and I are built the same way, and it isn't for emotional connections. But you can't deny our chemistry, and Charlie is a great kid. We're friends and that doesn't have to change. I provide the stability you need. Don't throw it away now."

She bit down on her lip and studied him, as if trying to gain control of her emotions. "I can't believe…" she began, but she was cut off when Sam's dad came up behind her.

"Sorry we're late," he boomed, taking Julia's hand and placing a loud kiss on her fingers. "You're looking fantastic as usual, my dear. So good to see you again."

Vera's gaze traveled between the two of them. "Is everything okay?" she asked, studying Julia.

The color had drained from Julia's face. Her eyes had grown large and shadowed. Sam wished he could pull her aside and finish their conversation. He got the feeling he'd made a huge misstep.

"We're fine," Julia said, taking a sip of water. She stood and hugged Joe then her mother. "Just working out details. You know."

Sam watched her gaze travel up and down her mother. "Are you all right, Mom?" she asked slowly.

"Never better," Vera said, smoothing her blouse.

"Why is your shirt buttoned wrong?"

Sam looked at his father, who had the decency to turn a bright shade of pink. Joe and Vera broke into a fit of giggles. Sam didn't know Vera well, but she'd never struck him as much of a giggler.

"I'll head to the little girls' room and adjust this." She swatted Joe playfully on the arm as she passed. "You old devil."

"You've got to be kidding." Julia followed her mother toward the back of the restaurant.

Joe took the seat across from Sam and gave him a hearty pat on the back. "How's it going, Sammy? Wedding stress getting to your girl?"

Sam's temper flared. "Finding out her mother is having sex with you might be getting to her."

Joe looked genuinely confused. "Really? I thought you two would be happy for us." A grin spread across his face. "Who knows, maybe we'll beat you to the altar."

"You've known Vera about a minute, Dad. That's not funny."

"Who's joking?" Joe opened his arms, lifting them toward the ceiling. "Some things are destined to be."

Sam needed a bigger supply of aspirin if he was going to continue to spend time with his dad. He pushed his fingers through his hair and took a breath. "Dad, tell me you aren't serious. I swear I'll throw you in the cruiser and deposit you at the state line if you keep talking like this. If you have an itch you want to scratch with Vera, that's one thing. But marriage? No way."

"Let me tell you something." His father leaned forward. "I'm not a young man anymore, in case you haven't noticed. I spent a lot of years sad and lonely after your mother died. Vera knows what it's like to lose a spouse. She knows what it feels like to be alone and crave something more."

"Vera is hardly ever alone." Sam shook his head. "She dates, Dad. A lot."

"From what I understand, you dated a lot before Julia. Did it make you feel less lonely?"

Sam opened his mouth then snapped it shut again. His father was right. All the women he'd dated when he first got to Brevia had just been passing time. He'd never felt connected to any of them. He'd always been on his own.

Until Julia.

"I'm going to ask her to marry me," Joe said. "It was love at first sight, and I'm smart enough not to let her get away."

"Do you think she'll say yes? I'd hope to hell she's smart enough to know not to be swept off her feet."

"What's wrong with being swept away? But don't worry. We won't plan a wedding until after you and Julia are settled. Neither of us wants to take anything away from you kids."

"That's so reassuring," Sam ground out. He scrubbed his hand over his face. "You don't have to marry her. Date for a little while. Take your time. Why rush into anything?"

"Life is short. It can turn on a dime. I'm taking every opportunity for happiness I can get. Just like you and Julia."

Nothing like him and Julia, Sam thought. This was a

disaster. His father's gushing romanticism made him look like an emotional robot.

He had to believe they were on the same page. She didn't want anything more from him than he was able to give.

Let his father rush blindly into marriage for love. It wasn't going to make him happy. If Joe hadn't learned that lesson from Sam's mother, Sam definitely had.

His plan was far more prudent. Enjoy each other but still protect his heart. It would be better for everyone in the long run.

The next day Julia cradled the phone between her cheek and shoulder as she sat in her office at the salon. She'd spent an hour staring blindly at the figures dancing before her on the computer and had made a call to an old friend to give herself a break.

"It's okay, Derek," she said with a sigh. "I'll figure it out."

"If those Southern belles get too much for you, I can always find a place for you in Phoenix. Everything's hotter out West, jewel-eyed Julia." Derek laughed at his own joke then said, "I've got to run, darlin'. My last appointment for the day just came in."

"Thanks, sweetie," Julia said, "I'll keep that offer in mind."

She hung up with Derek, a stylist she'd met years ago in Columbus. They'd both moved on from Ohio, but she still considered him one of her few true friends. For a brief moment she entertained the thought of taking Charlie and running away to Arizona. Not that it would solve her myriad of problems, but it sure seemed easier than facing everything head-on.

Julia drummed her fingers on the top of her desk, wishing she were out in the warm sun instead of stuck in the salon on such a gorgeous spring day. She needed to clear her head, and computer work wasn't cutting it.

What had started as a simple plan with Sam had gotten too complicated. She'd been stupid to think she could keep her heart out of the equation. If Julia were better at leading with her mind, she wouldn't have gotten into most of the trouble she'd had during her life. She wanted to be in control of her emotions. To be more like Sam, who could make every decision in his life based on rational thinking.

Not Julia. She was more a leap-first-then-look kind of person.

The only time that had worked in her favor was with Charlie. Now she'd even managed to mess up that.

Sam wanted to stay with her for the right reasons, at least on paper, but it felt wrong. His father and her mother were heading in that same direction on the express train. It had been torture to watch them last night at dinner, making googly eyes and barely able to keep their hands off each other.

She didn't realize it was possible to ache for a man's touch, but that was how she felt around Sam. Other than enough touching to make their fake arrangement seem real, they'd both kept their distance. Except when they were alone. In the bedroom, Sam was sweet and attentive and Julia had made the mistake of believing that meant something.

She pushed away from the desk and stalked toward the main salon. They were busy today, with every chair filled. She hoped to get the final approval on her business loan next week, needed to prove to herself and to the town and Jeff's family that she could stand on her own two feet.

Lizzy, the salon's longtime receptionist, stopped her in the doorway.

"Julia, could you take a look at this product order and make sure I didn't miss anything?" She shoved a piece of paper filled with numbers into Julia's hand.

Julia looked down as the figures on the page swam in front of her eyes. "Leave it on my desk. I'll check it over the weekend."

"I need to get it in before month end, which is today. It'll only take a minute. Please."

"I can't," Julia snapped with more force than she'd meant.

Lizzy took a quick step back and Julia noticed several customers and stylists glance her way. "Fine," she stammered. "But if we run out of anything, don't blame me." She turned away, ripping the paper from Julia's fingers.

"I'm sorry." Julia reached out to touch the woman's arm. "Lizzy, wait. I need to tell you something."

"That you're too dang important to be bothered by little details?"

Julia glanced around the crowded salon, her gaze landing on Lexi Preston, who watched her from where she sat with a head full of coloring foils. What was Jeff's attorney doing in her salon? Lexi blinked then raised one brow, as if in an odd challenge.

"I'm waiting," Lizzy muttered.

Fine. She was sick of hiding who she was, tired of working so hard to live up to her own unattainable expectations. She squared her shoulders and took a deep breath. "I have a learning disability."

"Come again?" A little of the anger went out of Lizzy's posture.

"I need time to look over the figures because I can't read them well."

"Since when?"

A hush had fallen over the salon and Julia realized everyone was waiting for her answer.

"Forever," she said, making her voice loud and clear. "I was officially diagnosed in third grade."

Lizzy looked confused. "I think I would have heard that before now. I was only a few years behind you in school."

Julia shrugged. "It wasn't public knowledge."

"Is that why you were always cutting class and getting kids to write your papers for you?"

Julia nodded. "I'm not proud of it. I was embarrassed and it made me feel stupid." She took a breath. "It still does. But I'm working on that. I hid behind a bad attitude and unkindness for a lot of years. I've changed. I don't want you to think I don't value what you're asking me to do. It just may take me longer to get it done." She swallowed down the lump of emotion crowding her throat. "That's my big secret."

Lizzy offered her a genuine smile. "My cousin was bulimic for most of her teenage years. She tried to hide that, too."

One of the customers tipped her head in Julia's direction. "My husband's addicted to internet porn."

"Oh." Julia didn't quite know how that related to her learning disability. "Well, I'll take these figures." She gently tugged the paper from Lizzy's hand. "I'll see if I can get through them this afternoon. If not, first thing Monday morning."

She looked around the salon one last time, her gaze catching again on Lexi's, and the lawyer gave her a surprisingly genuine smile. Head held high, Julia closed the door to her office. Once safely by herself, she leaned against it, bending her knees until she sank to the floor.

Her whole body trembled from the adrenaline rush that followed sharing her deepest, darkest secret with the ladies in the salon. Julia knew how the gossip mill worked in Brevia. Within hours, everyone to the county line and back would know about her learning disability.

The truth was that she no longer cared. Now that she'd talked about her disorder, its hold over her had loosened the tiniest bit. If people wanted to judge her or tried to take advantage of her, she'd deal with that. She realized she could handle a lot more when she used the truth to her advantage than when she tried to cover it up.

A little voice inside her head piped up, saying she might take that advice when it came to dealing with the custody case and Charlie's future. She quickly put it aside. Public humiliation she could risk—her son's fate she couldn't. Whether that meant keeping up the charade with Sam, or fighting tooth and nail with the Johnsons, Julia would do whatever she had to to keep Charlie safe.

Chapter Fourteen

"The Callahan brothers ride again."

Sam slanted Scott a look. "Who are you supposed to be, Billy the Kid?"

Scott grinned. "It's about time you stopped hiding in this backwater town and did some real work."

"I'm police chief, idiot. That is real work."

"If you say so. But it's nothing like being a marshal. You're going to love it, Sam. You won't have time to think about anything else."

That was a plus, Sam thought. He'd gotten the job offer early this morning. Scott had shown up at the station soon after to offer his congratulations. Sam was on duty, so they had coffee and a breakfast burrito in the car as Sam went out on an early-morning call.

His father was going to hit the roof. Joe had taken Vera down to the coast for a couple of days, so at least Sam would have time to formulate a plan before he had to explain what he was doing.

He had no idea what to say to Julia. He figured she'd understand. She'd tried to break it off last night. He knew their time together was at an end. After the custody ruling came through, she wouldn't need him anymore. Not that she ever really had. Despite her self-doubt, Julia was going to have a great life. He was the one who was hopeless.

Although he hadn't even thought himself capable of it, he felt his heart literally expanding every day with love for her and Charlie, but he couldn't make it work. He felt vulnerable, as if he was a moving target with no cover. He couldn't offer her anything more because he was too afraid of being hurt.

He'd spent most of yesterday working with Julia's attorney to file several affidavits on behalf of people around town attesting to Julia's character, her contributions to the local community and what they'd observed as far as her being a great mother was concerned. He knew she would never ask for help from anyone, let alone believe she deserved it. Once he'd explained what she was facing, people had come forward in droves to stand behind her.

He hoped that would be enough, would make up for what he wanted to tell her but couldn't find the guts to say. Instead, he was going to move on. Leave Brevia and cut his ties because that was easier than letting someone in.

"Before you go all bro-mance on me, you need to know I still think you're a jerk for what you did to me."

"You'll thank me eventually."

"I doubt that." Sam turned onto the long dirt road that led to the house he'd received the call about earlier. Strange noises, the neighbor had said. Here on the outskirts of town, Sam knew the parties could go on all through the night. He figured someone hadn't known when to let it go.

He shifted the cruiser into Park and turned to his brother. "If we're going to work together, there need to be some ground rules. The first is you stay the hell out of my personal life. It's none of your business. Even if you think you've got my best interests at heart."

"What are you going to do about the fiancée when you leave town?" Scott asked.

"I'm going to do her a favor."

"That's cold, Sam. Even for you. And I thought I was the heartbreaker. You're giving me a run for my money in the love-'em-and-leave-'em department."

"Don't make it a bigger issue than it is, Scott. She's better off without me. It's not going to work out. I'm not what she needs, after all."

"I can see why she'd be what *you* need, though. Her legs must be a mile long."

The hair on the back of Sam's neck stood on end.

"When did you see Julia?"

Scott gave him a hesitant smile. "Probably shouldn't have mentioned that."

"When did you see her?" Sam repeated, his knuckles tightening around the steering wheel.

"I drove down to have lunch with Dad last week. I needed a trim, so I checked out her salon."

"And her," Sam said between clenched teeth.

"After what Dad told me about how in love you are and the way you skipped out of breakfast to go running to her, it had me worried. I wanted to see what could be so flippin' amazing about this woman to make you all whipped."

"I'm not whipped."

"I was worried," Scott continued. "I put my butt on the line to get you this job. It wouldn't look good for you to flake before you even started. I have to admit, she'd be a big temptation. Her kid was there, too. Cute, if you're into the whole family-man scene. But I know you, Sam. That isn't who you are. Never was."

"Stay away from Julia."

"It's not like that. I told you that what happened with Jenny, I did it for your own good. Granted, I could have found a better way to handle things but..."

"You slept with her."

"I'm sorry, Sam."

Scott's voice was quiet, sincere. It made Sam's teeth hurt, because he knew his brother was sorry. He also knew that, in a warped way, Scott had done him a favor. At that point in his life, Sam had been so determined to prove that he wasn't like his father, that he could have both a career and a personal life, he'd ignored all the warning signs about how wrong he and Jenny had been for each other. She would have left him eventually. He would have driven her away.

Now he knew better, and he wasn't going to risk it again. Not his heart or his pride. He thought Julia understood him, but it was for the best that their relationship ended. As much as he didn't want to admit it, he was falling for her. He was close to feeling something he'd never felt before in his life, and it scared the hell out of him. What if he did let her in and she realized there was nothing inside him to hold on to? His heart had stopped working right the day his mother had died and he didn't know how to fix it.

Sam glanced at his brother. "Do you think about what would have happened if Mom hadn't been in the accident?"

"I used to," Scott said, a muscle ticking in his jaw. "But she would have divorced him, and the end result on us would have been the same."

"Yeah." Sam nodded. "I think Dad discovered his emotional self about two decades too late to make any difference in my life."

"You need to get out of here. Once you're working for the Marshals, you won't have time for all this thinking about your life. I'm telling you—"

Whatever Scott was going to say next was cut off when a stream of shots rang out from the house. "Stay here," Sam yelled as he jumped out of the car.

"Not a chance," Scott said, right on his heels, his gun in hand. "Call me your backup."

Sam gave a brief nod. "You go around the side," he whispered and headed toward the front of the house.

Julia dropped her cell phone back into her purse and took a deep breath. "I didn't get the loan," she said to her sister, the words sounding hollow to her own ears.

Lainey reached out a hand. The Tellett County courthouse was crowded on a Tuesday morning, and they stood near the end of the hallway, in front of a window that looked out onto the street. Julia thought it odd that the people below went about their business so calmly as her life spun out of control.

"Why not? What did they say? Oh, Jules, there has to be another way."

Julia shook her head. "They don't think I'm a good investment. It's me, Lainey. Nothing is going to change that. Everyone in the salon yesterday heard me. I told Lizzy about my learning disabilities. Clearly, the bank doesn't think I'm the right person to own my own business." She tried to smile but couldn't make her mouth move that way. "I can't blame them."

"I can." Lainey's tone was severe. "It's the most outrageous thing I've ever heard."

"Annabeth Sullivan is a vice president at the bank. I thought we'd come to an understanding and she'd forgiven me. I guess she still wants revenge."

"How long are you going to have to pay for your past mistakes? You're not the same person you were in high school. You've changed and everyone who knows you can see that. You're a good person. It's about time people gave you credit for how much you've accomplished."

"I haven't accomplished anything. The salon was my chance to make something of my life, to become more than what anyone thought I could." She scrubbed her hands over her face. "There's a reason I kept the LD a secret for so many years. It's easier to talk my way out of people thinking I'm stupid than to deal with the truth."

Lainey sucked in a breath. "Don't say that. You'll find another way. Ethan and I—"

"No. I'm not taking charity from you and Ethan, or Mom for that matter. Some things weren't meant to be. I've had enough disappointment in my life to know that." She glanced down the hall and saw Frank Davis motioning to them. "The hearing is starting."

"I thought Sam was meeting you here."

Julia swallowed back the tears that clogged her throat. "Like I said, I'm used to disappointment."

"Don't be silly. He'll be here."

Julia gave her sister a small hug. "Whatever you say, Lain. Right now, wish me luck."

"You don't need luck. You're a wonderful mother and that's what's most important. I'll be here when you're finished. We'll have a celebratory lunch."

The elevator doors opened as Julia walked past and she paused, her chest tightening as she willed Sam to materialize. When an older woman walked out, Julia continued down the hall alone.

She took her seat across from Jeff, his parents and their attorney. A small smile played around the corners of Jeff's mother's mouth. Lexi Preston didn't make eye contact, her eyes glued to the stack of papers on the table. A pit of dread began to open in Julia's stomach.

She darted a glance toward her attorney, who appeared blissfully unaware. But Julia could feel the long tendrils of impending doom reaching for her. She'd been in their grip too many times before not to recognize it now.

"Frank, what's going on?"

He looked up, a big smile on his face. "Didn't Sam tell you? He got a bunch of folks to write testimonials about your character. Really good, too. All of them."

Sam did that. For her. Then why did the Johnson family look so smug?

"Where is Sam?" Frank asked. "I thought he was meeting us here."

"Me, too." Julia swallowed. "I don't know what's keeping him."

The judge came into the courtroom. "In light of the new information given to me by both parties, I'm going to need a few more days to render my decision."

"What new information did they give her?" Julia said in a frantic whisper.

"Your Honor," Frank said as he patted Julia's arm reassuringly, "we aren't aware of any new information brought forward by the other party."

The judge slowly removed her glasses and narrowed her eyes at him. "Mr. Davis, you do know about your client's recent professional setbacks."

Frank threw a glance at Julia. "I'm not sure—"

"I didn't get the loan," Julia said miserably.

"We've spoken to a reliable source that tells us Ms. Morgan is planning to move out of the area." Lexi's shoulders were stiff as she spoke. "A colleague of Ms. Morgan's, Derek Lamb, had a conversation with her last week in which she expressed interest in a job with him at his salon in Phoenix."

Julia knew Lexi had somehow gleaned that information, as well. "I wasn't serious. I was upset about…about a lot of things, and Derek is an old friend—"

"An old boyfriend," Lexi supplied.

Julia shook her head, panic threatening to overtake her. "Hardly. I don't have the right equipment."

Frank squeezed her arm. "Be quiet, Julia."

The judge pointed a finger at her. "Ms. Morgan, your petition for sole custody was based partially on the stability of your current circumstances. Your ties to the community and your family being close were something I took into account when looking at your request."

"Her ties to the community are highlighted in the affidavits I submitted." Frank's voice shook with frustration.

"There is also the matter of her engagement," Lexi said, reaching over to hand a piece of paper to Frank.

Blood roared in Julia's head. No one could have found out her relationship with Sam wasn't real. They'd done everything right and she hadn't told a soul, not even Lainey.

Unless Sam…

She snatched the paper from Frank Davis's fingers and tried to decipher the words on the page, willing them to stop moving in front of her eyes. When they did, she felt the whole room start to spin.

"Were you aware," the judge asked, "that Sam Callahan has accepted a position with the U.S. Marshals Service in Washington, D.C.?"

Julia looked at the woman, unable to speak. Finally, she whispered, "No."

The woman's mouth tightened. "May I ask, Ms. Morgan, if you're still engaged to be married to Sam Callahan?"

Julia stared at the piece of paper in her hand, her vision blurring as angry tears filled her eyes. She blinked several times, refusing to cry in front of Jeff and his family. Refusing to cry over any man. "No, ma'am," she answered quietly. "I don't believe we are still engaged."

Frank sucked in a quick breath next to her. "In light of these new findings, I'd ask for a recess to regroup with my client."

"Yes, Mr. Davis, I think that would be a good idea. Our time is valuable, though, so please, no more wasting it. Get your facts straight and come back to me with a new proposal in one week."

"Judge Williams—" Lexi Preston's voice was clear and confident in the silence "—on behalf of my client, I'd like to request that you make your ruling today. The information that's come to light this morning is another example of Julia Morgan's inability to successfully manage her own life. It speaks directly to Jeff Johnson's concerns for his son and the reason he is here seeking joint custody."

Julia's gaze met Jeff's and he nodded slightly, as if to say "I told you so." Which, of course, he had. And she hadn't listened, convinced that this time events would work out in her favor. In large part because of Sam's confidence in her.

Sam, who'd encouraged her to go public with her learning disorder.

Sam, who'd promised to stay by her side until her custody arrangement was secure.

Sam, who'd betrayed her today.

Lexi cleared her throat. "I motion that you award sole physical custody of Charles David Morgan to Jeff Johnson."

The attorney's words registered in Julia's brain. They wanted to take Charlie from her. Completely.

She saw Jeff lean over and speak into Lexi's ear. The younger woman shook her head then glanced at Julia.

Julia felt the walls of the room close in around her. She looked at the judge's impassive face, trying to find some clue as to what the woman was thinking.

"Don't let this happen," she whispered to Frank. She needed to get back to Brevia, to wrap her arms around her son.

"We request you stay with your decision to rule next week," Frank said, his voice steady. "My client has been blindsided by some of these new developments. That in no way decreases her dedication as a parent or her love for her son."

To Julia's immense relief, the judge nodded. "We'll meet next Tuesday morning." She pointed a finger at Frank Davis. "Before that, I expect you to submit a revised proposal for custody. Remember, we all want what's best for the child, not simply what's easiest for one of the parents."

What's best for Charlie, Julia wanted to scream, *is to stay with his mother.*

She'd come into this meeting so confident. How could things have gone to hell so quickly?

She pushed back from the table. "I need to get out of here," she told the attorney.

"Be in my office tomorrow morning, first thing." His frustration was clear as he watched her. "This was a clear-cut case," he mumbled. "What happened with Sam?"

She bit her lip. "I don't know." What she did know was that Sam had left her vulnerable to losing her son.

Julia would never forgive him.

Chapter Fifteen

Sam ran his hands through his still-wet hair and straightened his shirt before knocking on Julia's door.

He'd stopped home for a quick shower after the mess this morning had finally settled down. An all-night party had turned into a domestic disturbance that led to a four-hour standoff. The homeowner, high on an assortment of illegal drugs, wouldn't let his girlfriend or her two kids out of the house. The situation had eventually ended with no injuries, for which Sam was thankful. But he'd been tied up in logistics and paperwork for most of the day.

He felt awful about missing the hearing and had called and texted Julia at least a half-dozen times with no answer. He'd then called Lainey, but she hadn't picked up, either. As mad as she'd be about him missing the meeting, the character affidavits he'd helped compile had to make up for it.

Sam couldn't wait to see the joy on Julia's face now that

Charlie was safe. He wanted to hear how things went, take the two of them to dinner to celebrate her victory. Even if she didn't want to be with him anymore, he'd make her see how important it was to keep up appearances a little while longer. He told himself it was good for her reputation but knew he couldn't bear to let go of her quite yet.

Julia deserved all the happiness life could offer, and Sam wanted to have a hand in helping with that before they ended their relationship. The thought of leaving her and Charlie made his whole body go cold. But he knew it would be best for Julia and that was his priority now.

He knocked again, surprised when Lainey opened the door. Even more surprised at how angry she looked.

"You have a lot of nerve showing up here," she said through a hiss. "She doesn't want to see you. You've done enough damage already."

The confusion of not being able to get in touch with her turned to panic. "Where is she? What happened?"

Lainey went to shut the door in his face but he shoved one gym shoe into the doorway. Lainey kicked at his toe. "I mean it, Sam. You need to leave."

"I swear, Lainey," Sam ground out, "I'll push right through you if I have to but I'm going to see her. Now."

Casper came up behind Lainey, barking wildly. Sam could see the dog's teeth shining and wondered if the dog actually meant to bite him.

"Casper, quiet." The dog stopped barking but continued to growl low in his throat. Lainey studied Sam through the crack in the door. "I'd like to call the cops on you."

"I can give you the number."

She blew out a frustrated breath and opened the door. Sam went to push past. "Where is she?"

Lainey didn't move to let him by. "I'm warning you. She doesn't want to see you ever again. She's in bad shape."

He shook his head. "I don't understand. Everything was lined up. Didn't Frank Davis submit the affidavits? They were supposed to make everything better."

"Julia didn't mention any affidavits. What she did tell me, between sobs, is that you'd told her to go public with her learning disabilities. For whatever reason, Annabeth Sullivan convinced the bank that she was a bad investment for the loan."

Sam's breath caught. "No."

"The best part, " Lainey said and poked her finger into his chest, "the part that really made all the difference, was the little bombshell that you've taken a job with the U.S. Marshals Service."

Sam's whole body tensed. "How did they find out?"

"You don't deny it? How could you have done that to her?" Lainey turned on her heel and stalked several paces into the small apartment.

"No one was supposed to find out until after she got the custody ruling."

Lainey whirled back toward him, keeping her voice low. "And that makes it better? You were her fiancé. A stable father figure for Charlie."

"Did Julia—"

"Oh, yes." Lainey waved an angry hand toward him. "I know all about your *arrangement*. It's ridiculous."

"I didn't mean for it to be. I wanted to help."

"You've put her at risk, Sam. At real risk of losing custody of Charlie."

"Where is she?"

Lainey stared at him. "In the bedroom," she answered finally.

"I'm going to fix this." Sam tried for confidence but his voice cracked on the last word.

"I hope you can."

He walked past her, Casper at his heels. The dog no longer seemed to want to rip off his head. Julia, he imagined, was another matter.

"I can make this right," he muttered to the animal. "I have to."

He knocked softly on the door, but when there was no response, he opened it. The curtain was pulled back, the room bathed in early-evening sunlight. Julia sat on the bed, her knees curled up to her chin, arms hugging her legs tight against her.

Sam stepped into the room and the dog edged past him, silently hopping up on the bed and giving Julia's hand a gentle lick before curling into a ball at her side. Without acknowledging Sam, she reached out to stroke the dog's soft head.

"Jules?"

Her hand stilled. "Go away," she whispered, her voice awful.

"Julia, look at me." Sam took another step into the room.

"I said go away." She lifted her head, her eyes puffy from crying, tears dried on her cheeks. She looked as miserable as Sam felt. He waited for her to scream at him, to hurl insults and obscenities. He wanted her to let loose her temper but she only stared, her gaze filled with the pain of betrayal.

Knowing it was his betrayal that had caused her suffering almost killed him on the spot. "I'm sorry," he began but stopped when she scrambled back against the headboard. The dog jumped up and stood like a sentry in front of her.

"I could lose him." Her voice was dull and wooden, as if she was in a pit of despair so deep she couldn't even manage emotion.

"You won't lose him." Sam said the words with conviction, hoping they would be true.

"You don't know. You weren't there."

The accusation in her voice cut like a knife through his heart. "It was work, Jules. I meant to be there." He sat down on the edge of the bed gingerly, not wanting to spook her or the dog.

"You're leaving."

"I thought it was for the best," he lied. The best thing that ever happened to him was this woman, but he was too scared of being hurt to give her what she needed. "That when you didn't need me anymore, it would be easier for us both if I was gone."

"I needed you today and instead I found out from Jeff's lawyer that you were taking a new job. You made me look like a fool, Sam."

The truth of her words struck him to his core. She was right. He was supposed to be there for her and he'd let her down. In a big way. It was the reason he knew he was destined to be alone: the work always came first for him. He was the same as his dad had been. It had cost his mother her life and now it might cost Julia her future with Charlie. He had to make it better somehow. "What can I do?"

She shook her head. "Nothing. There's nothing anyone can do. I have one good thing in my life. Charlie was the one thing I did right. And I've ruined that, too."

"You haven't—"

"I trusted you, Sam." As much as the words hurt, her voice, still empty of emotion, was the worst. "My mistake. I should have learned by now I can't rely on anyone except myself." She gave a brittle laugh. "And I'm iffy at best."

"Where's Charlie?"

"He's with Ethan. I couldn't let him see me like this." She ran her fingers through her hair. "I'm going to pull it together. I have to. But I needed a little time."

"We can get through this."

"There's no *we.* There never really was. You proved that today."

"I didn't mean it to end like this." He reached out for her again and Casper growled like he meant it.

Julia went rigid. "Don't touch me. I never want to see you again. I don't know what's going to happen with the custody arrangement. But I'll find a way to keep my son. He's all that matters to me now."

Sam shook his head. "Don't say that," he whispered.

Her eyes blazed as she spoke. "I thought you were different. I wanted to depend on you. I wanted to love you. Hell, I was halfway there already. It's over. I don't care what you say to your father or anyone in town about why this is ending. Blame it on me."

"This isn't over and I'm not blaming anything on you. If you let me—"

"I did let you. I let you into my heart and into my son's life and you betrayed us." She took a shuddering breath. "We're over. Whatever I thought we had is done."

"You can't be serious."

"Please go, Sam. Please."

He stared at her as she turned to the dog, petting him until he lay down again beside her. Sam wanted to grab her and pull her to him, hold on until she melted into him. This couldn't be the end.

He'd wanted to leave her happy, to do the right thing by her. Maybe he couldn't be the man she wanted but he'd been determined to see her through. To be the hero when it really mattered.

Now he was nothing more than the jerk who'd put her at risk of losing her son.

He stood slowly, his eyes never leaving her. He prayed she would look at him, give him some small glimmer of hope. When she didn't, he turned and walked from the room.

Lainey hung up the phone as he came down the hallway. "How is she?"

He shook his head. "She should never have trusted me."

"But she did, Sam. What are you going to do now?"

He thought for a moment then answered the only way he could. "I'm going to do what I do best—disappoint someone I care about."

Lainey looked as if she'd expected him to give some white-knight answer. But Sam was only good at playing the hero when the stakes didn't matter to him personally. When his emotions were on the line, he had a knack for royally messing up everything around him.

He walked out the door and into the dark night knowing he'd just ruined his best opportunity at a happy ending in life.

The image of Julia so forlorn would haunt him for a long time. Her anger and hatred might be deserved, but it hurt the most to know that he couldn't take away the pain he'd caused her.

For that, he'd never forgive himself.

Julia pushed the stroller along the plush carpet of the retirement home until she got to the common room that also served as a makeshift salon for residents.

"Good morning, Julia."

"Hey, Charlie."

Several voices called out to greet them, and she was thankful the people here were unaware of her personal turmoil, unlike most of the town. Charlie waved as though he was in a parade, which made Julia smile a bit. Her first in several days. She took a small sip of her coffee then placed it in the cup holder attached to the stroller's handle. It had been a rough week.

She tried not to show her emotions in front of Charlie, so she had spent a few sleepless nights crying in the dark hours and worrying about her future. The days were just as difficult to get through, since everywhere she went someone had a comment on her recent struggles. To her surprise, most of what people said had been supportive. Old friends and other locals seemed to come out of the woodwork to offer her a word of encouragement or commiserate on her situation.

Even Val Dupree, the Hairhouse's owner, had called from Florida to tell Julia that she was still willing to work with her to find a way for Julia to buy the salon. Julia had thanked her, but at this point she was afraid it was too little, too late. The Johnsons had so much power and she wasn't sure there was anything she could do to keep her future with Charlie secure.

Nothing mattered except Charlie.

She hadn't seen or spoken to Sam, although a couple of ladies had come into the salon specifically to tell her how they'd given him an earful about his reprehensible behavior toward her. Apparently, being screwed over by a man made you an automatic member of a certain girls' club.

If it wasn't for her constant worry about Charlie, Julia might be happy right now. For the first time in as long as she could remember, she felt as if she was a true member of the Brevia community.

But everything else faded when she thought of her son and what she'd need to do to keep him with her.

Before moving forward with her plan, she had this one last loose end to tie up.

"Good morning, Mrs. Shilling," she said as she walked into the room.

"Well, hello, dear." A gray-haired woman, sitting at the games table with a deck of cards, lifted her head and smiled.

"Hi, Iris." Julia directed that greeting to the younger woman wiping down counters at the back of the room.

"Hey, Jules. Thanks for coming on such short notice." The younger woman waved at Charlie. "Hey there, Chuckie-boy. Do you want to check out the fish while your mommy helps Mrs. S.?"

Charlie bounced up and down in his seat. "Fishy," he squealed. "Charlie, fishy."

"Thanks, Iris." Julia picked up her coffee from the stroller and pushed the buggy toward Iris. She always brought Charlie when she came to Shady Acres. The residents and employees loved seeing him.

As Iris left with Charlie, Julia turned to the older woman. "Mrs. Shilling, where did you find the scissors?" She stepped forward and ran her fingers through the spiky tufts of hair on the top of the woman's head.

Mrs. Shilling placed her hand over Julia's and winked. "In the craft cabinet, dear. They forgot to lock it after our art class yesterday."

Julia opened her bag and pulled out a plastic apron, spray bottle, scissors and a comb. "What do you think if I clean it up a little? You've done a nice job here, but I can even up the sides a bit."

"I suppose," Mrs. Shilling answered with a shrug. "When I was a girl, I had the cutest haircut, just like Shirley Temple. I wanted to look that cute again." She met Julia's gaze, her hazy eyes filled with hope. "Can you make me look like Shirley Temple, dear?"

Julia patted Mrs. Shilling's soft, downy hair. "I'll do my best." She wrapped the apron around the woman's frail shoulders. "Next time, go easy with the scissors, Mrs. S. You're beautiful just the way you are."

She usually came to Shady Acres every other week to cut and shampoo the hair of a group of residents. But Iris had called her last night to say that Mrs. Shilling, one of her favorite ladies, had butchered her hair. Julia made time to come here before she needed to be at the salon.

She used the scissors to snip a few tendrils of hair as Mrs. Shilling hummed softly.

"Everything okay in here?"

Julia turned, shocked to see Ida Garvey walk into the room.

Mrs. Shilling's face lit up. "Ida, so nice to see you here this morning. This is my friend Julia. She's making me look like Shirley Temple." She glanced at Julia. "This is my daughter, Ida. She's a very good girl." Her voice lowered to a whisper. "She still wets the bed sometimes. Has nightmares, poor girl. I let her snuggle with me until she falls asleep."

Julia gave a small smile. "Nice to see you, Mrs. Garvey."

The older woman shook her head. "I haven't wet the bed since I was seven years old. The Alzheimer's has affected my mother's memory of time."

"I figured as much. I won't be long here."

"They called to tell me she'd cut her own hair again."

"If she ever wants a part-time job, we could use her skills at the Hairhouse." Julia continued trimming the woman's fluffy hair.

"She can't do any worse than some of those girls you've got working there."

"Play nice, Mrs. Garvey. I've got the scissors."

One side of Ida's mouth quirked. "She talks about you a lot."

Julia glanced up. "Really? Me?"

"In fact, I have a suspicion she might have done this just to get you out here again."

Mrs. Shilling pointed a bony finger at her daughter.

"Children are supposed to be seen and not heard, young lady."

"I'm almost seventy, Mom."

"Still holds true," the woman said with a humph. "Besides, she's going to make me look like Shirley Temple. Or maybe Carole Lombard."

Julia smiled, something about this woman's affection lifting her spirits the tiniest bit. She was grateful for every lift she could get right now. "I was thinking Katharine Hepburn, circa *Adam's Rib.* Gorgeous but spunky."

"I'll take spunky," Mrs. Shilling agreed and settled back into her chair.

"I heard about your recent troubles," Ida said, her gaze assessing. "What are you going to do about the salon?"

"My loan wasn't approved. What else can I do? I'm not sure if I'm going to be in town for much longer, actually." She squeezed Mrs. Shilling's shoulder. "I'll miss you when I go."

The woman heaved a sigh. "All the good ones move on." She gave a watery smile to her daughter. "Except Ida. She's my best girl. Always has been."

Julia's chest fluttered at the love in the older woman's gaze when she looked at her daughter. She suddenly saw crotchety Ida Garvey in a new light. Julia knew she'd look at Charlie like that one day. She'd do anything to keep him by her side so she'd have that chance. Nothing was more important to her.

Ida gave her mother an indulgent smile, and then with her customary bluntness she asked Julia, "How did the bank deal get messed up?"

Julia pulled in a deep breath and paused in her cutting. "They didn't think I was a good investment, I guess." She paused, squaring her shoulders, and then said, "As you've probably heard, my learning disabilities are severe. Not exactly the type of applicant you'd trust to run a business, even a small local salon. Too bad, though. I had big plans."

Mrs. Shilling clapped her hands. "She told me all about it, Ida. Getting rid of that horrid name. She's going to offer spa services. I want to bathe in a big tub of mud!"

"Is that so?" Mrs. Garvey asked, looking between her mother and Julia.

Julia gave a small laugh, embarrassed now that she'd confided so much in the older woman. "My idea was to make it a destination for people traveling in the area and the go-to place for a day of pampering for women around the region. There's really nothing like that unless you head over to Asheville or down to the coast."

Ida nodded. "Tell me about it. I've put most of the miles on my car driving back and forth for a monthly facial."

Julia felt color rise to her cheeks, embarrassed she'd shared her dream now that it wasn't going to come true. "That's probably more information than you wanted for a simple question." She used a comb to fluff Mrs. Shilling's white hair. "There you are, beautiful." She handed her a small mirror. "Katharine Hepburn, eat your heart out."

The woman smiled as she looked in the mirror then at her daughter. "Do you love it, Ida?"

"I do," she agreed.

Julia removed the apron and took a broom from the supply closet in the corner. "I'll have one of the girls come out to do your hair when I'm gone." She began to sweep up the hair from around the chair.

"Ida, give her some money," Mrs. Shilling ordered.

Mrs. Garvey pulled her wallet from her purse.

Julia shook her head. "I don't charge for my time here."

Ida took out a business card and handed it to Julia. "This is the firm that handles my financial portfolio. The president's contact information is there."

Julia took the card. "Oh." She knew Ida Garvey's late husband had left her a sizable inheritance.

"If you decide you want to stay in the area and are still interested in investors for your business, call him. I see the need for the type of spa you're describing. I assume you have a business plan our loan team could review?"

Julia nodded, dumbfounded by the offer.

"Good. I don't want to pressure you. I don't know why the bank here didn't approve your loan, but I'd guess it had something to do with Annabeth. That girl isn't the sharpest knife in the drawer. But I certainly hope it wasn't because of your learning disorder. It doesn't make you a bad bet for a loan."

"Thank you for saying that."

Mrs. Shilling reached out and took Julia's hand. "Ida is rich," she said in a loud whisper. "She takes good care of me."

"You're very lucky," Julia told the woman, feeling a tiny flicker of hope that her own luck had taken a turn for the better.

Chapter Sixteen

Sam hit the mute button on the television and jumped off the couch, throwing on an old T-shirt in the process.

His heart soared at the thought that Julia could be the person insistently knocking on his front door.

He groaned as he opened it to reveal his father and brother standing side by side on his front porch. "Not now, boys," he said and went to swing the door shut again.

His dad pushed it open and knocked him hard in the chest. "What the—" Sam muttered as he stumbled back into the house.

"That's what I'd like to know." Joe's voice was hard as he stalked past Sam. Gone was the gentle emotion of his recent visit and in its place the tough, take-no-prisoners Boston cop had returned. Sam wanted to be grateful but knew what it was like to be on the receiving end of his father's temper. His own fuse felt too short to deal with that right now.

He glanced at his brother, who shrugged and stepped into the house, closing the door behind him.

"What the hell were you thinking?" Joe bellowed, slamming his palm against the wall. "You took advantage of that girl. You used her to deceive me and now you've deserted her. That's not how I raised you. I've never been so angry and disappointed in all my years."

Angry and disappointed? Even in the midst of a full-blown tirade, Joe was talking about how he felt. Sam had damn near had enough of it.

"This is your fault," Sam countered. "If you had left me alone, none of this would have happened." He squared his shoulders, warming up to the subject, needing a place to vent his own anger. "You came in here, emotional guns a-blazin', and wanted me to turn into somebody I'm not. It's never going to happen, Dad. I'm never going to be some heart-on-my-sleeve kind of guy, spouting out my feelings and crying at sappy chick flicks." He pointed a finger at his father. "You raised me to ignore my emotions. It's what you made Scott and me into after Mom died. I can't change. The mess I made of things with Julia is proof of that."

"You faked an engagement," his father interrupted, hands on hips, matching Sam's anger.

"It was wrong. I know that now. The alternative was you following me around waiting for unicorns and rainbows to come spewing out of my mouth. It ain't going to happen. Ever. Julia and I had a business arrangement and I messed it up. If I could go back and change things, I would."

"No, you wouldn't."

Sam and his father both turned as Scott spoke for the first time.

"You don't know anything about me or what I would do," Sam spat out. "Neither of you do."

"I know you," Scott countered. "I know that girl got

too close. She got under your skin, and I bet it scared the hell out of you. It sure would have me. With her big eyes, long legs and cute baby. She made you feel things and the Callahans don't like to feel." He nodded toward Joe. "Another gift from you, Dad. I don't know what she wanted or expected from you, but it's a good thing you ended it when you did. We don't do love. We're not built that way."

How could his brother be so right and so wrong at the same time? Being with Julia and Charlie had scared him. But it was because he realized he did love her even though he'd tried to ignore, then bury, his emotions. He'd fallen hard and fast, and it had made him want things that could never be.

She wanted someone to be a father to Charlie. Sam's paternal relationship was so dysfunctional it was almost laughable. How could he be a decent father with the role model he'd had in Joe?

What if he tried and failed with Julia? He was capable of love, but not in the way a woman like Julia deserved.

Suddenly Joe fell back onto the couch, clutching at his chest.

"Dad!" Both Sam and Scott were at his side in a second.

"What is it, Dad?" Sam asked.

"It's his heart, you idiot."

Joe's eyes drifted closed, and Sam moved his head and legs so he was lying flat across the cushions. "Call 911," he ordered his brother.

Scott pulled his cell phone from his back pocket, but Joe's eyes flew open and he reached out a hand. "No, I don't need medical attention."

"The hell you don't," Sam said on a hiss. "Make the call, Scott."

"My heart hurts," Joe said, his voice trembling, "because of the pain I've caused the two of you." He lifted himself to his elbows and looked from Sam to Scott. "My sons, I've failed you and I'll never forgive myself for it." He covered his eyes with one hand as sobs racked his shoulders.

"Of all the…" Sam grumbled and sank to one arm of the sofa.

Scott threw his cell phone on the coffee table and stalked to the front window, grumbling under his breath.

"Scoot over, old man." Sam sank down on the couch next to him. "You just about gave *me* a heart attack there."

"I need a drink." Scott's voice was tense.

"Make it three," Sam told him. "There's a bottle of Scotch in the cabinet next to the stove."

Joe still sat motionless, other than an occasional moan.

Sam's headache spread until his entire body hurt. "Dad, pull it together. It's going to be okay."

"Do you believe that?" Joe asked finally, wiping his damp cheeks. "Do you feel like you're going to be all right without her?"

No. Sam knew his life was going to be dark and dim, that he could spend years chasing the adrenaline rush that came with his career and nothing would compare with the excitement of having Charlie call him Dada. He felt as though he could be a hero to hundreds of nameless people, and it would pale in comparison to coaxing a real smile out of Julia.

"What choice do I have?"

"You always have a choice. That's what I didn't realize until recently. I had a choice to let your mother's death practically kill me, too, or to keep living. I didn't do a very good job of making my life count until recently. But I'm learning from the mistakes I made and doing my damnedest to make them better. You have a real chance for love with Julia. Take it."

"What do I have to offer her?" Sam asked quietly, finally getting to the real heart of the matter. His own fear. "She deserves so much more."

"I know you think that, son. But if there's even a glimmer of hope, you've got to try. Hell, you've got to try even if there isn't. Because what you have to offer is everything you are. It may not feel like it's enough but that's for her to decide. If you never put it out there, you'll spend your whole life feeling empty and alone. Trust me, that's no way to live."

What if Sam opened himself up to try? He may not feel as if he had enough to offer, but he was certain he'd work harder than any other man alive to make her happy. He wanted to see Charlie grow up, to be there for every T-ball game and skinned knee. He wanted to watch Julia hold their babies and grow old with her and everything that came between.

She was everything he'd ever wanted but was too scared to believe he deserved. He nodded as resolve built deep within him. "I've got to talk to her."

"You'd better get moving, then. She's got a head start on you."

Scott walked back into the room, balancing three glasses of whiskey. "Turn on ESPN and let's drown your sorrows."

Sam ignored his brother. "What do you mean 'head start'?" he asked his father. "Where did she go?"

"According to Vera, Julia took Charlie and headed to Ohio this morning. They caught a flight out of Charlotte. She told her mother she had some kind of a plan and needed to talk to the ex-boyfriend before the final ruling."

Sam's head spun. All he could think of was that Jeff had offered to marry Julia—some sort of business deal where Julia would come to Ohio to raise Charlie near the grandparents and they'd pay all the living expenses. Not a real relationship, but it was no better than what Sam had offered. And it would end the custody battle once and for all.

How could he have been stupid enough to let her go? What if she wouldn't take him back? What if she figured Charlie's father was a better deal?

Sam had to stop her. He loved her with his heart and soul. His life would be incomplete without Julia and Charlie in it, and he'd fight as long and as hard as he could to win them back.

He jumped off the couch and grabbed his keys and wallet from the side table. "I've got to go," he yelled to his father. "Lock up behind you."

Scott grabbed his arm as he strode past. "Don't do this. No woman is worth running after like you're some cow-eyed schoolboy."

"You're wrong," Sam answered, shrugging him off. "Julia is everything to me. Someday I hope you'll find a woman who makes you want to risk your heart. You deserve that. We both do. Dad's right. He messed up after Mom died, but we don't have to repeat his mistakes. I've got a chance to make it work and you'd better believe I'm going to take it."

"What if it's too late?"

"I've got to try."

Scott shook his head, disgust obvious in his angry gaze. "You have to be in D.C. tomorrow at eight o'clock sharp. You're going to make it, right?"

"I sure as hell hope not."

Scott cursed under his breath. "Idiot," he mumbled and drained his glass of Scotch.

"Sam."

Sam turned to his father. "I'm going to make it work, Dad. You know how relentless we Callahans can be."

"Good luck, son." Joe smiled at him. "I'm proud of you."

Scott snorted and picked up a second drink. "You go turn in your man card. I'm getting drunk."

Sam wanted to shake his brother, to open his eyes the way Sam's had been, but he didn't have time. His only priority right now was Julia and getting to her before she made a deal with Jeff Johnson.

"Sam?"

He turned to his father, who threw a small, velvet box in his direction. Sam caught it in one hand. "Is this…?" His voice trailed off as emotion overtook him.

"I had it sent down from Boston. Your mother would want you to have it."

He nodded. "Thanks, Dad," he said on a hoarse whisper then sprinted out the door.

"You've got a lot of nerve coming into my home uninvited." Maria Johnson looked down her nose at Julia. "Watch your child," she barked suddenly. "That's an antique Tiffany vase."

Julia leaned forward to pick up Charlie, who had toddled over to a wooden table and reached up to rub his tiny fingers on a glass vase perched on top.

"Hi, Mama," he said. His gaze went to Maria, who scowled at him, causing him to bury his face in Julia's neck.

Julia looked around the formal sitting room where a housekeeper had led her. It was cold, sterile and, like the rest of the house, totally inappropriate for an energetic boy. Even now she heard Maria *tsk* softly when she noticed the fingerprints Charlie had left around the bottom of the vase.

She'd asked for Jeff, but he was on his way back from a round of golf with his father. Unwilling to be distracted from her mission, or maybe afraid she'd lose her nerve,

Julia had insisted on being let into the enormous house. She'd known Jeff's family had money when they'd dated, but the *Dynasty*-sized home gave her a much better perspective on how rich the Johnsons really were. They clearly had unlimited resources at their disposal to get what they wanted.

Which brought her back to the matter at hand.

"I still can't believe you have the nerve to try to take my son from me," she said with a dry smile. "I guess that makes us even."

"Your case is crumbling, and you lied about your relationship status. It's only a matter of time until they take him from you. It will be better in the end. We can give him so much more than you could ever dream of. Look at Jeffrey."

"Speaking of *Jeffrey,* he asked me to marry him."

Maria didn't speak but the anger in her eyes said it all. Her face remained as smooth as marble, her expression typically blank, thanks to one too many cosmetic procedures. "Why would he do that? We don't need you to raise the child properly."

"Maybe giving a kid every material thing they want doesn't cut it. Your son is a loser, truth be told."

"How dare you! He's a respected professor with—"

"Funny, I thought that, too, when I first met him. Turns out, Jeff is a bit of a joke around campus. He does his research expeditions, conveniently funded by your husband's corporation, but little else." Julia sat Charlie on the floor and gave him several plastic toys from the diaper bag to keep him occupied. She dug through her bag for a stack of papers. "I have written documentation from the university about the sexual-misconduct charges filed against Jeff by four different undergraduates. Apparently, when he was teaching, it took a bit of extra work to get an A from Professor Johnson." Julia didn't mention that three of the incidents had happened during the time she'd been dating Jeff.

Maria tried to narrow her eyes, but they only moved a fraction. "How did you get those?"

Julia wasn't going to say where because she honestly didn't know. She hadn't even known until this moment whether the information she'd been given was real or fake. She'd been desperate, racking her brain for a way to make the custody battle go away, even wondering if she actually should accept Jeff's horrible proposal for Charlie's sake.

Then, two days ago, a package had arrived for her at the salon, containing the information about Jeff and other sordid details regarding the Johnsons.

At that moment, Jeff and his father walked into the room.

"What's she doing here?" Dennis Johnson said through his teeth.

"Julia, have you finally realized my offer's the best you're going to get?" Jeff gave her a wink and a sneer. To think she'd once found him attractive. She'd been such a fool. Charlie threw the set of plastic keys then went to retrieve them. Both men looked at him as though he was some sort of flesh-eating alien. There was no way she was going to let this family get their hands on her son for one minute, no matter what she had to do to prevent it.

"Jeffrey, be quiet." This from Maria. "Thanks to your on-campus dalliances, Ms. Morgan thinks she has some hold over us."

Jeff's voice turned petulant. "Mom, I didn't—"

"Sit down, son." Maria's voice took on a dictator-like quality and Jeff's mouth clamped shut. "You were groomed for so much more. We gave you everything." She pointed to the damask-covered couch. "Sit down and let your father and I fix this problem like we have all your others.

You've messed up things for the last time. We've got another chance with your son. I won't let you get in the way."

A sick pit grew in Julia's stomach as Jeff's shoulders slumped and he threw himself onto the couch. She'd known he didn't get along with his parents and now she understood why. She wondered how many of his problems were thanks to being raised by Mommy Dearest's twin sister.

Julia might have problems, but she knew she'd always put Charlie's best interests first in her life. Which was why she straightened her shoulders and said, "Jeff's not the only one in the family who has trouble keeping his parts in his pants." She waved a few more papers toward Dennis. "Like father, like son, from what I've discovered."

Dennis swallowed visibly as Maria sucked in a harsh breath. "How do you know that? No one has that information. I paid good money to make sure of it."

"Not enough, apparently." Julia picked up Charlie, who was grabbing at her legs. "Now let's talk—"

The door to the sitting room opened and Sam burst through, followed closely by the Johnsons' housekeeper.

"I'm sorry, ma'am," the older woman said, gasping. "He barged right past me."

Sam stood in the entry for a moment, looking every bit the bull in a china shop. Oh, how she loved him, even now. Every part of him. Julia's heart seemed to stop for a second. Charlie squirmed in her arms at the sight of Sam, squealing with delight. Julia hated that her body had the exact same reaction.

"The fake fiancé?" Jeff drawled from the couch. "Really, Julia? This is a bit of a production, even for you."

Sam pointed at Jeff. "Shut your mouth, pretty boy, or I'll come over and do it for you."

"What are you doing here, Sam?" Julia asked, her voice hoarse with emotion. She didn't want to need him. She didn't want to need anyone but was so relieved to not be fighting this battle alone, she could barely hold it together.

He looked at her and she knew he saw it, saw everything about her. He knew she had a tough exterior but was soft and scared at the core. And she knew it was okay to be vulnerable around him, that he wouldn't judge her or use her weakness to his advantage. Even with all that had happened between them, she ached to trust him. To lean on him and use his strength as her own.

"I'm here because at your side is where I belong. Forever."

"Don't bother," Maria said with a sniff. "There's no audience. The judge isn't here. No use pretending now, Chief Callahan. It's too late."

"That's where you're wrong." Sam took a step forward. "At least I hope you're wrong. Is it too late, Jules?"

"For what?"

"For me to be the man you want and need me to be." He walked toward her then bent to his knee. "For this." He pulled a small box out of his pocket and opened it, a diamond flanked by two emeralds twinkling up at her.

Julia and Maria gasped at the same time.

"It was my mother's ring. I want you to have it." He smiled at her hopefully. "I want all of it, Julia. You and Charlie and me. I love you. I want to spend the rest of my life proving how much. Proving I can be the man you deserve."

"What about the U.S. Marshals job?"

"I called today and said I wouldn't be joining them. The Brevia town council has renewed my contract for another three years. I'm there for keeps, and I want it to be with you. We're going to make this work. I'll be at your side fighting for Charlie, for our family, as long and as hard as it takes. Just don't give up on me, Julia."

Confined to her arms long enough, Charlie practically dived forward toward Sam, who wrapped his arms around him. “Hey, buddy. I’ve missed you.”

He took the box from Sam’s hand. “Here, Mama.” Perched on Sam’s knee, Charlie held the ring up to Julia.

She held out her hand, and the two men she loved most in the world slipped the ring onto her finger. “I love you, Sam. Always have. You had me at the car wreck two years ago.”

He straightened and wrapped both her and Charlie in a tight hug then kissed her softly, using the pad of his thumb to wipe away the tears that flowed down her cheeks.

“This doesn’t change anything,” Maria hissed. “We’ve got all the time and money in the world.”

“But don’t forget the information I still have. I don’t want to use it but I will, Mrs. Johnson. I’ll do anything to keep my son safe.”

“That won’t be necessary.” Jeff stood, looking as thoughtful and serious as Julia could ever remember.

“Jeffrey, stay out of this.”

“Not this time, Mother.” He took a step toward Julia and Sam. “I don’t want to be a father. I never did. But I can tell you that my son deserves better than what I had growing up.”

“You had everything,” Dennis argued, his face turning bright red.

“He deserves a family who loves and cherishes him.” Jeff’s gaze never left Julia. “Have your attorney draw up the paperwork for me to relinquish custody and send it to my office at the university. I’ll sign whatever you want me to.”

“No!” his mother screeched.

Julia felt a lump form in her throat as Sam placed a

calming hand on her back. "Thank you, Jeff. You won't regret it."

One side of his mouth kicked up. "When it comes to funding my next research trip, I may. But I'll take that risk. Good luck, Julia." And with that, he walked from the room, followed quickly by his parents, screaming at him the entire way.

"Too 'oud," Charlie said, covering his ears with his chubby hands.

Sam's arm was strong around her shoulders. "Let's take our son home," he whispered against her ear. "We've got a wedding to plan."

* * * * *